Louisiana

Louisiana

A NOVEL

by Erna Brodber

University Press of Mississippi

First published in 1994 by New Beacon Books Ltd.
First published in the United States of America in 1997 by University
Press of Mississippi

00 99 98 97   4 3 2 1

The paper in this book meets the guidelines for permanence and dura-
bility of the Committee on Production Guidelines for Book Longevity
of the Council on Library Resources.

Library of Congress Cataloging-in-Publication Data

Brodber, Erna.
  Louisiana : a novel / by Erna Brodber.
     p.   cm.
  ISBN 1-57806-031-1 (paper : alk. paper)
   1. Afro-Americans—Louisiana—Folklore—Fiction. 2. Women
anthropologists—Louisiana—Fiction. 3. Jamaican Americans—
Louisiana—Fiction. 4. Young women—Louisiana—Fiction. 5.
Supernatural—Fiction. I. Title.
PR9265.9.B75L68   1997
813—dc21   97-21363
                                                CIP

To :

Uncle Bertie
Uncle Joe
Papa
Michael Cooke
G. Beck
Dung Wing
who successfully challenged my view of geography.
We read you loud and clear.

Contents

Prologue

Editor's Note

Franklin D Roosevelt, (may his tribe increase) faced with a depression cast hither and thither for schemes to reduce unemployment. He created jobs for plumbers, architects, the unskilled. Bless his sweet heart, he also created jobs for artists. His WPA provided gainful employment for many writers black and white, male and female. Ella Townsend was one of those up and coming black women writers the project employed. She was to retrieve the history of the Blacks of South West Louisiana using oral sources.

Ella Townsend disappeared leaving a blotch on her name. This promising writer, for whom they had even procured a fellowship in Anthropology to upgrade her fieldwork skills, was one of the few to be given the new field aid, an approximation of today's tape recorder. Neither recording machine, reel, transcript nor manuscript was submitted. Was Ella Townsend a petty thief, incompetent? The rumor was that she had disappeared with a confidence trickster into store-front fortune-telling in receptive New Orleans.

In the early 1970's, nearly forty years after Ella Townsend's descent into the unknown, this manuscript called *Louisiana*, then as now, appeared on our desk. Its arrival was well timed, perhaps well planned. Our small black woman's press, like all other publishing houses was looking for works on and of black women. One found us. The package in which this manuscript came, carried a Chicago post mark. It had been recently posted. There was no other identifying mark. It was our feeling after reading this manuscript and still is, that Ella Townsend's husband who may or may not go by the name mentioned in the work, deposited it with an attorney, possibly his friend, with the injunction that it should be sent to the 'right' publisher at the 'right' time. He did well. We thank him. It continues to be our feeling too, based on our reading of the manuscript that Ella's husband went (back?) to the Congo and possibly died in the Kasavubu/Lumumba struggles of the 1960's.

We have not spent time verifying the existence of all the parties mentioned in this manuscript. We stopped at Ella Townsend. She did exist. Her last publication according to our research, appeared in *Crisis* Vol XLVl1 1935. We have also found evidence that she was one of the writers employed to the WPA, so be she in her last days petty thief, conjure woman, anthropologist, we do know that she started public life as a writer and was employed officially as such. We know too that whatever her life became, certainly included diary-keeping at which exercise she performed creditably if erratically — some evidence of scientific intent and action.

The text argues persuasively that Ella came under the influence of psychic forces. Today the intellectual world understands that there are more ways of knowing than are accessible to the five senses; in 1936 when Ella Townsend received her assignment it was not so. The world is ready. We are. This manuscript's arrival is opportune. And in more than one way.

Here in *Louisiana* is a mixture of social history and out of body experiences, perhaps a new field of study. What the world needs now? We have subjected it to little editing. What looks like part of a letter, accompanied this manuscript. It is the closest thing to the usual covering note that is attached to a manuscript. It talked about the disposal of Ella Townsend's body and the writer's plans for his future.

4

We accept this as a note written by Ella's husband and possibly sent originally with the work to the attorney, friend, or whoever it was that relayed it to us. We have appended this note as an epilogue, using its last sentence as a heading, in line with the style of the rest of the work. This is our major intervention, mandated we think by the distinctly communal nature of this offering, an approach which is most obvious towards the end of the manuscript. Here a voice, which we presume to belong to Ella's husband, appears.

The text came to us divided into six parts — 1) I heard the voice from heaven say 2) First the goat must be killed 3) Out of Eden 4) I got over 5) Louisiana and 6) Ah who sey Sammy dead. Is there a message in these titles, we asked — I heard the voice from Heaven say, "first the goat must be killed (and you get) out of Eden and get over (to be) Louisiana." Den a who sey Sammy dead, (if this can happen). A hypothesis. We called the epilogue, our appended note from Ella's husband(?), 'Coon can', to complete this thought/hope, entering by this act into the community of the production.

The manuscript arrived in 1974. No one has yet contacted us about rights or remuneration. Acting within what appears to us to be a community purpose and orientation to this work, we will, with the royalties from this book (assuming no one comes forward to claim them), begin the Ella Townsend Foundation for the study of commonalities in African America and the African Caribbean in the period between the World Wars. Our press extends the chain of hands. Join us. Interested parties may contact us.
E.R.Anderson
The Black World Press
Coral Gardens
Miami Florida 20067   March 1978

I heard the voice from Heaven say

Anna do you remember? Can you still hear me singing it?

It is the voice I hear
the gentle voice I hear
that calls me home?

They sang it for me Anna. They sang it for me, and Anna,
had I any doubts about how they saw me and that in
coming home I had done the right thing, I could now lay
them to rest along with that crumbled old body to keep
which in one piece had taken too much from too many
people these past four years.

Upon the hill
the rising sun,
they sang and I couldn't help but add my own tone deaf
notes to that song I still love so, sang in a way I still love so,

It is the voice that calls me home.

My song Anna. It has no written score. Succeeding
generations of us, on each of our occasions have, like you,
simply appointed their own tenor, their own alto, their own
timing to descant and fill out gaps built into a score by those
who wrote it.

It is the voice I hear
That calls me   home
          calls me
I hear them say "come unto me"
It is the voooice that calls me home,

making fifteen minutes out of a three minute piece, a flyingsaucer out of a John Crow blow nose — I once drew that for you Anna — a compact disc out of that soft perforated red fungus.

And they were all there. Every jack one of them I had told you about was there to celebrate my translation. They came in carts and every scrammie there was; they came through short cuts with their shoes in their hands; up shalley hillsides with nothing but coconut oil on their feet. They came in groups; they came alone. They came with banners: Mizpah 1, Mizpah 2, Mutual Association Benefit Society, Daughters of the King, Brotherhood of St Andrew, Ethiopian Burial Scheme no.1, their velvet banners in the brightest reds and blues, the words embossed in opposite colours, tassels flying; they came in long white gloves; they came with swords; Ezekiel's boom-boom band with the round white faced drum, pulling itself up the hillside by sheer faith.

White is the funeral colour here as there. Against the green of the trees, the black of their skins, the vibrant colours of their banners, it telescoped one loud clear report, 'Hail Aunt Louise', I could cry. Anna, I was seeing every corner of that scene. Being translated is like that. You can see from every angle. And I tell you. What a sight! Like so many clean white birds nestling in a Portland thicket — parish beside mine, remember — shaded by the flowering mulatto companion tree. And the singing. Vox populi. *I hear the voice, the gentle voice.* Is the voice of God. *That calls me home.*

That voice calling me home truly did come in a whirlwind, Anna. Shepherd taking your hand on the moaning line and twirling on and on until every face is nothing but the vapour rising from your asphalt road on a hot wet day. Then only the voice, Suzie Anna, carrying you now in the chute, the voice with you now in the chute, keeping you company

10

through the waters, over the rainbow's mist, into seventh heaven and back to fete through days of dinkie mini, to see this thanksgiving and the nine-night to come and without a tired muscle. Back with every faculty — all hands, feet, eyes, ears a body could need for higher service.

Den ah who sey Sammy dead.

Two

Been sitting here and thinking Lowly girl, Lowly girl. Rocking and thinking Lowly girl. Been rocking and thinking of you Lowly girl and that rainbow in the mist. Them heavy black braids is gone Lowly girl. Thin schmuck now left, Lowly girl. Just this old red rag twixt me and the sun and this scattered old brain Lowly girl.

Woman been here just like you, sounds like you. Done changed colours on me Lowly girl? And them fine long legs and this knife seamed slacks, what's that about Lowly girl? Been crossing the sexes up there Lowly girl or managed to merge man into woman? Don't think I can't see you, St Peter's mail man, message basket where a gold watch had been.

–Mammy King–

You here again Lowly and I had heard you that time. Back cross the sea to your bitty old island, how was I with only these hands, these feet and that fat head of hair, with Silas, two fading blooms, three units to set up, to do more, to find strength to sail cross the seas to see people like birds lowering a pine box into six feet of earth, and singing that song that you always sang whenever you braided my hair? Huh!.

Three times I did see me on that rainbow with you... when I went to get water and fell into the water... the fits never

11

left me you know. I saw that banner like a large hair ribbow and the master's hands open to me. But not yet. Silas' needs jerked me back. Donna Claire all but took me to you Lowly girl but Madam Marie's prayers came between us that time. Then Silas came back from that Arkansas devilment with something fit to drive us all home. He left but I stayed, to help the kids make it and what are they now? Dew swallowed by sun. Am sitting here rocking and thinking, this old red rag barely keeping these scattered dry brains from turning to raisins and I am thinking this young woman, is it you Lowly girl, come to usher me home for I'm tired and lonely and want to come home.

–Mammy King, you over there? You think you should be sitting in the sun with just that thin handkerchief on your head? Sun will dry out your brains Mammy King and I need them. Hold on to me. I'm going to move you and your chair to the shade and then we are going to sift through those brains.–

That's right Lowly girl.

–Close your eyes Mammy King and go back in time as far as you can.–

That's right Lowly girl, though you no how would have called me that then. Suzie Anna, you liked to say. "Suzie Anna, where you got that heavy engine hair from? Reminds me of my grandmother." "She pretty", I would say, "Ain't want no one favouring me less and if they be pretty".

–I'm putting this tube round your neck... remember we talked about that?... so I can get into my black box here all that you have in that head you're so determined to dry out in the sun.–

Victrola, Lowly. And 'Coon Can' it was. Remember the first

12

time you heard that black box and that dreadful rag song spewing from it, your skin caught a fire and your already hot head was all set to burst. Miss Inquisitive had peeped into the Mister's room... that he was then... "Nobody singing Miss Anna", you whispered...that was then too and I was only 'Miss Anna'... "but there is singing and playing". Little green gal from the islands. "Victrola honey", I said. Now coming to tell me 'bout her black box.

–Mammy I'm reading your face. You're back there already. Didn't need to ask you to go back. Now take me with you. Tell me what you see, tell me what you hear and what you feel.– Same old Lowly. Reading face. What you used to say then? "Your face my thane is as a book where men may read strange tales." "What you talking 'bout little green island", I would say. "Your face Miss Anna. You are nowhere here. You run away gone from this cold. Take me with you Miss Anna." And I'd laugh: "Ha ha".

–Two ha's are better than nothing,– the girl said to herself of that runaway laugh as she leaned her chair forward willing my Anna to share it with her and her new-fangled black box.
"That's all you have to say Miss Anna? One little laugh?" "They ain't teach you nothing at school little green chile? I hardly get no schooling but if you ask me to count, I could make it to two and I did count two laughs, didn't I?" I would try to get you off of my case and on to anything else. "Get out of my face sunshine and mind the mistress' plates." But who could shut you up? "Just like my Granny I tell you", you'd go on. "Every little thing is the biggest of secrets. But neither you nor she nor anyone else can keep light from shining through their eyes, nor keep their muscles from moving when their selves need to speak. And I can read face, you hear me Miss Anna. I soon read all about

13

your home down in the South. And it is down South."
Child glance up and must be she vision that lazy old sun
trying to mess with the ice round my heart for she say, "Yes
I'm right and I shall be more right. Going to ride there with
you. Watch out, I'm coming." "Child", I tell that funny-
talking child, "they teach you much where you come from.
You can sew real good, you talks real good and you can
cook, but ain't nobody teach you to button your lip?" I
feared they might take my sunshine away and bury her in
that kitchen downtown. Child don't even know mens!

Anna sighed another sigh that leaked from our history and
the girl made a note to be sure to find some way of
transposing those sighs and those laughs and other non-
verbal expressions of emotions into the transcript she would
submit to her masters. –And I'd better do that indeed for it
seems,– she said quietly and matter-of-factly to herself,
–Mammy will give me nothing else to add to these white
people's history of the blacks of South West Louisiana.–

Child hold on to that little sigh I sigh. "I know what you
thinking Granny Anna. I can see it in your face: what's up
with that nosey Thomasina and the goings on in that
room?" T'was the one thing could calm you. Questions
'bout goings on in Silas' room. Island baby saying quietly,
"And you know what? I'm going to tell you all about it and
soon". What to do with that child? That child and that
room? I have eye, mistress have eye. Messing with the
lodger! They bound to send that little green thing down to
that no count kitchen. Nothing I could do but be the
granny and all them island kin folk she say I so favour,
though I be no more than twenty years older than her.

The child wrote down Anna's silence in her head as 'full
thick and deep'. –Recording machine–, she said to herself,
–I need braille to access those thoughts.–

14

Three

They teach Green Island 'bout Helen and Helena... see
some of your pointless matter did stick in my head. One is
a lady; the other an island. They teach you about Perseus,
Agamemnon, Clytemnestra, Persephone, Daedalus, Andromeda, sounds that have no right sitting together, yet they fall
off your tongue so easy like fresh water down a clean man's
back, like the satisfying goings on a good wife don't mention
and they did make my heart full. But Green Island, they tell
you nothing 'bout a place called Louisiana right here in
these united states of America. who laughs last... so Green
Island jaw drop; Green Island now quiet. Sea lashing stone
gone still like a cemetery; like the silence of the night when
the Christ was born.

"You not from Louisiana, Miss Anna?" Green Island know
nothing but New York and Chicago and a place called 'the
South'.
"Sure right I am babe and mighty proud of it, Miss Green-
Island-Gone-Quiet, though things be the way they be that
have me up here though I'd rather be there." Salt physic
and senna for little green island.
"From St Mary's parish, Louisiana. Yes Mam." Green
Island one open-mouthed duck gagling on my little bit of
water.
"You not from Louisiana, St Mary, Miss Anna."
"Cross my heart and hope to die. Born and bred there
Mam. Mammy from there, Pappy from there. Go ask
fearless Ramrod, waiting by the cotton tree. Go ask him,
he'll tell you, 'I pitch my tent, I make my nest, I hatch my
seed. Ain't going no place. Gotta swing me right here. St
Mary Louisiana's where I intend to stay.' And they did
swing him right there. So hey there little green island, you
ain't the only soul got a place called 'St Mary, Louisiana'."
"So Miss Anna, you knew all the time and never let on."

15

"The big master name me Grant, Mam. Never said Brook nor River nor Sea nor any of them chattering things beating itself 'gainst this poor black stone that yearns for some peace and cannot get none, for it is tied to its babbling in this white woman's kitchen."

Green Island gone quiet. One of them Greek gods done stole up and stole all the sound from that island, must be.
"Cat got your tongue, Miss-Quiet-Green-Island? Ain't nothing more make you quiet before save talk 'bout you in that Mister's room. And I tell you again, green girl from Louisiana, St Mary, Jamaica, with much book-learning and little horse sense, you don't know men, you don't know mistresses. Don't mess with the mistress' boarders. She will send you right back to that convent you run from." Talk 'bout the Mister and that room, could close you off tighter than an old woman's chest and send you sailing the skies for a safe place to land, but this was a silence in a class by itself. This was a boil gathering its parts to break loose. Green Island is a carbuncle oozing all over my skin.

"Miss Anna, you are my family. My mother was a Grant. Her grandfather a Grant. All Grants are my cousins. They all born and grow where I come from."
"Well ain't that something! Two places make babies. Which is the Mama and which is the Papa. Holy Father married them, Green Island?" But it was passing strange and I'd been studying the matter since the day that I found out. You do know that Lowly, and here is that woman come to mell me again.

Ah who sey Sammy dead. Ah who sey Sammy dead.

–Considering woman, here you are sitting in the sun again, drying the substance from your brains. Don't dry them out yet Mammy, I need them.–

"Mammy, Mammy, Mammy. This Mammy business. Lowly this ain't you. No how you would be into this 'Mammy-Mammy' for so long. So who is this kid that looks just like you and sounds just like you and comes bothering me just like you used to?"

"Whose hair is that Anna? Though you hardly can tell with it pressed out so straight. Whose bottom is threatening to unbalance whose legs like a train on a rickety track?"

"They did tell you at the convent, you tell me, just how ladies should walk. News caught me too late but I got by somehow. Still, who is this gal with some bits of me and some bits of you?"

"Two places can make children! Two women sire another? Who laughs last... Could be your chariot. Hold tight Suzie Anna. Get those water-logged feet to swing off the ground."

"This be the kid?"

"This is the horse. Will you ride?"

"Will she do?"

"Best I have seen. Will you ride?"

"Let's see if she will."

−Mammy I see you looking at me full and smiling. Like you are ready to talk. Just let me take you out of the sun. Now, see this red button. It is pushed right down to record what you say. After about an hour, it will jump up with a ping. Don't let it worry you. It just means that we will have used up one side of the spool. Just keep on talking while I turn it. And Mammy, what we want to know, to be truthful, what those people want to know, but as it happens, I want to know too, is what life was like for you, so go right back and tell me all about Louisiana; tell me about leaving Louisiana; why you chose Chicago; how it was settling into Chicago and how and why you came back to settle here. Tell me anything, everything.−

17

Four

The young lady leans over and smiles her smile thinking that with that speech, her fine line black pen and with her red button depressed, she has loosed Anna's threads and the ravelling would start. But that fabric is self-edge and on all of its sides.

–Child who you be?– Anna says as she flicks the first card from the pack, shuffled, cut and waiting on the imaginary board that joins their knees into a lay-away card table.

–Me? Yes. That's a good question. You should want to know who is messing with your brains. I'm studying, sort of, at Columbia– says the child searching her hand, arranging it into potential tricks, and those preliminaries done, thinking it did make sense to discard that one spade.

–What you studying at child?– Anna takes up that card.

–Your children and grandchildren... have you anybody studying?– Good move, good move but it is Anna who smiles for that card is a seven and she already has the jack.

–Everything in its time. Yes child, what you studying at? What you aiming to be?–

–Oh Mammy, what am I studying? Anthropology, Mammy.– The child draws from the pack. Nothing of note, so she throws out another card from her pitchy patch hand. –And I'm also a writer and that's why they thought I'd be good for this job.– And out goes another in the hope of something better from the adversary's hand. –So shall we now pick through those brains and put what's in them in my hungry black box.– But this isn't the whist her youngman had taught her. This is coon can and Anna, with time on her hands, had mastered the skill in the longshoreman's strike and had honed it to fine art on Chicago's Southside.

–Where do you come from child?– Anna trips in, distracting the girl. –You really do talk in two different ways. Can't

18

figure it.—
—From New York, Mammy.—
—New York don't talk so. Where before that?—
—Nowhere really Mammy.—
—'Really'. Meaning what?—
—My parents.They are from the islands.—
—Huh. Lots of them little bitty islands down there. And yours got no name.—
—Jamaica. Mammy—
—Yes. That is right. And that's why you sounding so very much like her. Both of them girl?—
—Yes Mammy—

Anna quickens her pace. She is totally in charge.
—I know that place from listening child. Now whereabouts your parents come from?—

The child sees her opening, her chance to take over. To take it or not to take it. She knows Anna is building a suit made of clubs. If she plays jack-seven-six, then Anna will know that she doesn't have the queen, and already wise to the fact that she doesn't have the king can throw her completely. This is thin ice and she's never got further than lacing the skates. If she lets her know now, how little she knows of the land of her parents, Anna might close up for she really is fixed, so she thinks, on dealing with that and where would go then the little exchange that had started to grow. The truth is deceitful; it will out and embarrass you, so out comes:
—Mammy this is going to sound like I'm trying to shut you up but it is the truth. I left Jamaica when I was an infant. My parents had already migrated. They came back for me. They don't say very much about the place that they came from.—

Child could have saved herself planning and thinking for Anna continues to pull tricks from her sleeve.

19

—Mighty strange child. That Lowly did talk so! Then who you was with there? You don't keep in touch?—

—My mother's mother but she died. That's probably why they came to get me.—

—They have high science there.— Anna presses on again, hogging the game. —They didn't tell you anything about that, my child?— And doesn't wait for an answer. —They rebellious folks, them Jamaican racemen. One feisty fighting lot, they seemed to me. They have brass bands but not as good as ours; they have mento, flat-footed shuffle like ours; they have pukkumina, that's what they call getting the power; they have tobacco and some sugar cane but no cotton. They have bananas in banana trees like windmills. 'By and large', that's her word, your trees are not straight; they tend to have branches sticking out of their sides and you can sit on them like on benches. You have green turtles too.— And Anna, my poor Anna, burst into song.

Green turtle sitting by a hole in the wall
hole in the wall, hole in the wall
Green turtle sitting by a hole in the wall
looking at the deep blue sea.
Green turtle look so lonely, reminds me of me
Guess he's thinking 'bout his little girl turtle
Sitting somewhere in the blue.
And I haven't see my Bodinya in a long long time I know
But I'm sailing home
Just as soon as the winds from the old West Indies blow.

She really did love that song so! She awaits no applause. Just continues:

—And you have no winter. But you have plenty rain just like us here. And sometimes hurricanes. Lowly caught pneumonia in one of them. Held on for four years doing her part of the work but it took her straight home. Never felt the big quake. 1907. That was big! Bodies on top of bodies.

She didn't actually see that but she did see the warner in full dress regalia for she had been in the market just the week before that. She didn't see the frogs jumping hop scotch in and out of the earth as it opened up now one crack, now the other. But she heard of it.–

My ancient mariner simmers to a close.
–I would love to have been there to see all those things she talked about. "You can read", she said. They had helped me with the reading. "I can write. I will write." But you never did. Not in that way Lowly girl. Your handwriting is pretty, ain't gainsaying that but your voice Lowly girl, could travel like lightning carrying pictures of the sun, of the rain, of the sound of the rain on the roof, of the one-sided grin of a neighbouring child. My ears can pick up a story... how well you know that. Four years of pain and then you sailed out to happiness.–

The recording machine goes 'ping' and the girl is Hamlet again; whether 'tis nobler to turn the tape over and to go on or just throw the towel in.
–One whole side gone–, she thought, –and not a thing to give to the white people. How would it look? This woman they say has important data to give; is important data; she has seen things; had done things; her story is crucial to the history of the struggle of the lower class negro that they want to write. I was chosen to do her. It was an honour. Because of my colour, I could get her to talk. Because of my colour, she treats me like a daughter to whom she gives orders. Because of my colour, I have nothing from her but orders on this reel. What can I tell them? How is this going to look?– Without further ado, she bends over, manoevers her black box into its case, puts her arm through the strap, and it on her shoulder, takes her bag from the shoulder of the chair that she sat on, put that too on her shoulder, slaps her anger in neutral, for anger it is, and quietly says:

–Venerable Sister. This is a bread and butter matter. My name and my job are at stake– and makes to step off with that, disrespectful of scientific procedure, of closing the interview neatly and leaving a lead for the day thereafter, thinking it is more prudent to admit failure to them than to have them discover it. A null lead is still a lead and Anna you are seizing it.

–Little bread and butter and 'them' is all you can think about?– The thing is now personal and certainly unscholastic. Hear you now Anna:
–"Man shall not live by bread alone".– Hear our girl now: –"but by every word that proceedeth out of the mouth of God", first temptation, but... –
Hear you again Anna before the child can finish her sentence:
–Don't say it child. Don't say you are not the Christ.–
Exasperated and defeated, how else to react but to limp away with what of one's dignity that can be retrieved! The child adjusts the strap on her shoulder and walks. It is you, Anna who reach out:
–See you tomorrow.– The child smiles. The baby is turning. You push, sensible Anna.
–Machine's mighty heavy. And so is your bag. Leave it with me and stop puckering your brow. Jack Johnson my neighbour's grandson is a fine young man. He'll take it to you.– The little scientist is as happy as a lark. Our headwater is breaking.

Five

–Do you remember how it was for us Anna?–
–More like a sheet of ice cracking in that Chicago kitchen. Then was when I knew for sure that all that Greek and Roman and fast and plenty talk was just one big fur coat lifted from them books for warmth.Girl child cold! Ain't

lived through nothing like Chicago cold. Burn them mountain of books you done read and it ain't amount to two minutes of warmth. Not one thing to hold on to! Child just turnip bush rooted, caught in an icicle and thawing, one tiny wingless rat bat fallen from a hole in the roof. Collapsed. I had thought with all them visits to Silas' room you hadn't seen what you should see. More fool me! And I was hard with you. "Who can't hear bound to feel", I did say. But you didn't get the point. Naturally, for that weren't the point. "I didn't have no choice", you say. 'Didn't have no choice'? Island baby saying, "'Didn't have no choice'? Old school teacher dead?" I say inside my head. Aloud I say "Hmm", deep and sharp, John Henry's hammer hammering a warning. Hm, that hammer don't even thud in your ears. That ain't where it is at. "Father say go, I go." "Call him father", I say within my head. "You're right. Man old enough to be your father. Faded photograph!"

"They were good to me and they are right, I can make it here. It's just this cloud and this cold. Sometimes I feel I am locked in a white ice cube."

—Well I sure feel like a dog. Child homesick and cold and all I can think of is what I think go on below that poor man's belt!—

—You apologised—

—Yes. 'Fess up and apologised. You turned around. I could see your backbone stiffening, your head settling itself on your neck. You tackled that basin of dirty dishes and pans and when next you spoke I was just 'Anna'. And then our good times rolled.—

—And they will roll again—

—Yes. Feisty enough. High spirited yet humble—

—Yes. She will do.—

Six

The kid overslept. How could she sleep so with that fat head of wire. Rushes, with that heavy machine at ready, to find you sitting in the sun, only this thin scarf on your head, just as she told you you shouldn't, hands on the arms of your chair trying to make for the rainbow, disregarding due process. Hold on to your horses Anna. You're teasing her so! Child touches your fingers and you give her no answer, as if you've given her much answer before! Puts her hands on top of yours. Why did she do that? Thank God. At last Sue Ann. Does she know what she is doing? Child thinks you have died and rushes for Forbes.

The girl walked home with your smile Anna. And then again, it might even be 'in'. 'With', 'on', 'in', they were all in there. Your puckered lips were her grandmother's knees. And she thought; withered muscles make a warm blanket that falls around you, caresses you, not pressing you like meatier thighs do. Soft, pliant and warm. Her Granny, she remembered, had had a little stool with a back made for her. Sitting on this, a sea of penny royal perfuming the air, behind them the green interior of their house, the wash stand with its green basin and goblet both with red flowers at the sides, one sitting inside the other like Granny and she, one's knees open to receive the head, then gently, very gently first with the tip of the big-round toothed comb, unknotting the ends of the hair, then with the fingers of both hands, taking that plait apart, going through the six plaits made some days ago. Almost sleeping, her head moves with the motions of grandmama's hands and Granny locks her knees tighter to keep this precious parcel from slipping, from nodding too far back and hitting its head on the edge of the floor where her larger frame sits. Granny is wordless, leaving her space to wander over to grandfather's tomb, to the bead flowers around it, to the huge kitchen near it, up with

Granny's pee, into the lata, into the oven, through the zally, carefully down that path past the waterhole, carefully, for that is wet stiff clay and you could slip, back under the tangerine tree to look over the side of the hill and on to the field full of bamboo sticks with light green yam vines creeping on them and back up to the barbecue where Mr Bonner, that poor peeny wally lives in his bottle. Round edges of the comb massage the scalp. Grandmama parts. No more than six strands at a time, parks the comb in loose hair, examines each strand, dips a finger in the sun-warmed castor oil and massages the scalp. Now and again, between changes of action, between the parting, the searching, the dipping of the finger, the massaging, the kid returns to watch her grandmother and then to fly away again and to feel Granny slowly shuffling off, patting her back and taking her to her cot. Some old ones never learn. For hardly has she deposited this precious bundle to her crib before it is up, standing, holding on to those firm bamboo legs, babyface between old knees and she must gather her up again, back to her chair, back to her seat on the floor and back to the plaiting of the hair. "Chicken I was sure you were sleeping", the old one says every time. "No Granny" she says, "just flying with my eyes shut", but Granny doesn't hear. She knows her baby can't talk.

The girl heard herself say, "I'm flying", jerked herself into the present and said to herself, "That serial dream of the old lady again", and felt relieved that she had avoided the sensation of falling that always came with that dream. Strong-willed girl, she had stopped in flight by pushing herself into the present and had missed the chance of knowing that the time was here when we would keep her afloat with our knees.

Our girl last evening walked home with you Anna but only part way. A golden boy came to take her to Chimboraza,

Cotapaxi and Pococataptl as well. Girls will be girls, so she sailed right past the knowledge to straighten the house... there's so little time for such things in an up and coming academic's life... to prettying herself, for marrying him is part of her plan and this boy needs hearth as well as a beautiful woman, she thinks. But for this Reuben and her sense of his needs, she'd have continued her brown study with, in and on your smile, as on her way home; seen nothing, heard nothing, a cart led by a horse; been suspended with us and learnt once more how to fly without fear and been ready much earlier to take you on home. Man in the head Anna, but girls will be girls.

'Stead of doing as she ought to, budding research worker they think her to be, checking the machine the boy brought her and reviewing the day, our daughter finds her straightening comb takes it to the kitchen, lights her little oil stove, waits for a blue flame, stands the comb on its back in it and with her hair divided into the portions her grandmother once searched, greases the strands with a sweet smelling oil, presses the back of the comb to the roots of the bunch. Her ancestry satisfactorily neutered, she sits herself down to wrapping small bundles of hair over bits of covered wire taken from her patchwork hair-tidy. With her head now fat with bits of coloured wire, she ties a scarf on it and turns back to housewifing.

Chops up the onion and garlic and commits them to a covered dish lest they make of her hearth a mere kitchen; seasons the chicken pre-plucked by a neighbour, and to keep the drudgery of house work from clinging to her person, soaks her hands in a basin of water, liberally sprinkled with the essence of peppermint. Self-esteem needs a triumph a day and Anna she couldn't really pat herself on the back for making an old lady reel out her life story, so she earned herself credits by getting a bath and a douche in the wooden wash basin of the labourer's cabin the programme director felt would put her in the informant's environment and help her to formulate the right kind of questions.

The beautiful lady inside and out, preparing her beautiful hearth for her beautiful lover, changes and powders the sheets. Southern fried chicken! Frying smells in a love nest! No. That will not do. With nothing but a stove top, it's pot roast for that bird. So with infinite care so that no onion or escallion or garlic could sully, she transfers the seasoned chicken to an iron pot, covers it up and sees it to a slow fire. No need to hurry: seasoning could slowly and decidedly enter meat to make a succulent meal for her Reuben. The hurry would have to be, come tomorrow when she'd have to get to you Anna, her flirtatious old lady, get back home to deposit her things and be off with her to Franklin to collect her Prince Charming. There would be little time to freshen up so what was done tonight had to be done well to last into tomorrow.

The effort was somnambulistic. The kid overslept and rushes here to find you like this. "Mammy just died" and out come the if's. "If only I hadn't overslept; if I had had my priorities right." "No problem" you say. "Just tell the white people the old lady has died." You frightened her deep down this time. Have the child thinking she's spoken aloud, for your lips aren't moving. It couldn't be the health worker, the poor child is thinking for she doesn't know her problem and in any case, Forbes is only now bustling down the steps in her usual delayed sympathetic way, worrying about the trials of the world and asking her would she babysit you while she goes off for the doctor and for the manpower to get you to bed. "Lived past her time", Forbes says for the nth time. "Going off every other day. Won't let it go, yet telling her friend just as often, 'I want to come over the rainbow's mist'!" Dear Forbes wouldn't know. Any day now. The head has presented.

Ah who sey Sammy dead

The child knows they are not her words for they are nowhere in her head but she is quite sure that she has heard them and that your lips haven't moved. With so many years of formal schooling, she cannot think 'ghost'. Ventriloquist, she thinks. "Can the old flirt", that's you Anna, "have this too in her past?" Anna when will you stop teasing! At death's door as in life?

–Them teachers did teach you nothing 'bout living; they teach this one nothing 'bout dying or passing the lifeline. Ain't know what she did.– She knows that she heard that. Not just thought she heard that.

Ah who sey Sammy dead.

There is no question about it; it is as clear as a bell. Somebody spoke. A voice very familiar and it isn't her Mammy's. The ears are hearing other frequencies. The child has come through. Anna, she'll make it.

First the goat must be killed

The above is as true and exact a transcription as I Louisiana, the former Ella Townsend, now Kohl could with guidance over the years manage to make of my first encounter with my teachers. *"Ah who sey Sammy dead."* They had placed that message in my head. It was my voice that kept saying it, though nowhere was that phrase in my consciousness at the time. I now know that it is the refrain of a folk-song from home but I didn't know the song, having left there at an early age and my parents, wishing to dissociate themselves from some aspect of their past did not/would not have sung such a song nor would they have kept company with people who would sing such a song. Nevertheless the voice that uttered these words was inescapably mine, less recognisable at first but finally leaving me and Reuben who listened too, with no doubt of my involvement with the exchange, though the total extent of it I did not share immediately with him. What are the qualifiers suitable for what I would admit? — 'Unconscious involvement?' 'Subconscious involvement?'. Nothing I had read had prepared me for the notion of thought transplant or whatever name we give to it. Thank God for Reuben. But for him I might have handed myself over to a psychiatrist. It was he who pointed out to me that I hadn't heard any more voices than he had; that the voices on the reel were there for all to hear and verify; that the only singular experience I had had was of saying things of which I feel I have no knowledge and that I should wait and watch before committing myself to a path that could label me mad or at best odd. I let myself be comforted by that momentarily. This was a position he held even after he had heard all.

I had worked very hard at building that little rapport with Mammy that you feel in the transcript. I could not afford to jeopardise it. At the same time I did not want the people's recording machine to hurt its head. That would be embarrassment plus. I from nowhere was one of the first to be given this instrument, this precious instrument, first of its kind, donated to the programme by the manufacturers. I argued however that a recording machine, given to me as much for use as for testing, could more easily absorb hurt and be repaired than a relationship and so left it to be carried home in accordance with Mammy's suggestion, by the trusty Jack Johnson. And it was true. What they say of me as recorded in the transcript is true: I didn't listen to the reel. I checked that it was in place, spool intact, nothing at all out of order and pressed on with my planned programme.

Reuben was coming next day by train then by bus to somewhere he'd never been before; we were meeting for the first time in two months. I did love my work and was in seventh heaven that Mammy had become so open and engaging with me and I walked home for at least half of the way, it is true, with her but Reuben's impending visit naturally took over my thoughts, so that by the time the chap came, I had quite left the history of the Negro of South West Louisiana and was with my chap. And thank God for those few moments.

They let me arrange the house, pretty myself and allowed me some extra sleep. By the next morning, November 11th 1936 I was no longer just me. I was theirs. The venerable sisters had married themselves to me — given birth to me, — they would say. I could feel the change. There was that morning and after, no doubt in my mind that I had heard things that nobody had said to me and that I had said what

I could not have said but what I was to hear myself say thereafter so often when they were about to make contact with me or when I needed to speak with them, — *"Ah who sey Sammy dead".* It was, and even more so now, is my opinion that the surrounding environment speaks miles about the interview and I had developed the habit of turning on the machine as soon as I entered a site and I did do that, that morning on entering Mammy's space and had kept it open even when there was nothing for my ears but her silence. I did that again on the morning of her collapse. Rushed over and without even thinking, turned on the machine.

Whatever had happened with me, however, had apparently happened from the first day of machine recording Mammy. As you can see from the transcript, my other self entered their space as early as that — involuntarily — shortly after Lowly sang her song. A truly tone-deaf lady! I did not hear her speak or sing; I did not hear me think; I do not recall even feeling odd or that anything odd was going on. Nevertheless, the machine pulled out those words, that thought, out of me and in my voice. By November 11th, as I have already said, the sense of having spoken was emerging. This was the morning of Mammy's fainting. I had spent some minutes with her before Mrs Forbes' interjection and I had had the sense that my mind had been spoken aloud. Mrs Forbes left us to go fetch the doctor. There is no doubt at all in my mind that during her absence I said those words that are foreign to me and I sensed that I was a party to conversation between others. I was more that just frightened. I was shaken to the roots.

I am here an adult, in my late 20's, my own and sole breadwinner. Running away is not an option open to me. I was on the job. I had no choice but to stay where I was until company came and with that, the imposition of sanity upon this odd situation. The doctor was not long in coming.

33

I gathered from him that Mammy was in another of her fits and that these were normal for her. He merely put the thumb and the index finger of one hand in the sunken area of her cheek and with the other yanked her mouth open and put a spoon which he summoned Mrs Forbes to bring, crossways under her tongue much like a bit rests in a horse's mouth. That I gathered was to stop her from biting her tongue or somehow swallowing it and choking herself. And he did inject her. Through all of this, he muttered that he didn't see why Mrs Forbes who was hovering at the back and leaving me in the foreground as if I not she was in charge, could not with the help of a neighbour do all of this, instead of wasting his time and wasting the old woman's insurance money.

He obviously had time to spare notwithstanding, for he hung around chit-chatting with me until Mammy was sitting up and her old flirtatious self again. I waited until the doctor pronounced her recovered before taking my leave for Franklin, my journey home, my love and my powdered sheets. Which sheets didn't get a chance. We were hardly home before the said Jack Johnson was back at my house to say that Mammy had died: really gone this time.

* * *

My Reuben is still an active student of Anthropology, and more authentic than I, having passed all the requisite stages preliminary to the award of a doctorate, having seen field work in his native Europe, and in Ceylon, while I have been slipped into formal studies sideways on the experience clause, ably supported by the absence of others of my race to step forward. We both like social investigation and easily switch gears from pining lovers to scientists faced with an exceptional challenge. Oral report is out, so what next? Make use of the situation. On to the study of funeral rites. We made ourselves "head cook and bottle washer" — one

34

of the few phrases from my mother's island past that she allowed herself — in preparation for Mammy's final journey. I myself have no doubt at all that I did shout out, and I mean shout in the church, *"Ah who sey Sammy dead"*. Reuben says I kicked, fought, foamed, stared, had to be taken from the church and given water. I knew nothing of that. Reuben wasn't teasing and he doesn't lie. I know nothing of that. I know that I was in a kind of grotto.

The water in St Mary's parish, Louisiana flows down embankments protected by thick growths of shrubs. You walk across a grassy lawn to get there. That's not where I was, though my place bears some resemblance to it. I was at a place that had added something to it and had subtracted something from it, that had edited the St Mary bayou. Instead of the sleepy stream going on and on to where you lose actual sight of it but know that if you walk further down you will see it, here were rocks willy nilly in the water and a mound of irregularly placed ones as if hastily called upon to protect the mouth of a cave — no down stream here — and out of it came a wide rainbow, growing like an adjustable ladder across the sky. I swear I saw Mammy, whom I cannot now in my mind call Mammy for she was a spritely young woman with braids about her head. I saw her there. She was humming as, one hand over the other, she climbed the ladder over the horizon and across the sky. It seemed, as it does even now in the telling, quite the normal thing to do. What held me was the way her white dress took on the colours of the rainbow as she ascended. I watched her vanish into, absorbed into the sky and looked around to see the horizontal boards of my cabin's window, my pillow, my hands on my sheet, smell the powder on those sheets and see Reuben's worried eyes. I closed my eyes again. This time it was a deep dreamless sleep.

The house was as quiet as Juliet's tomb. Reuben is a man

of action, a great organiser and beautiful in a crisis. I knew that he had not deserted me but had gone off to do something which would have some positive bearing on our present situation. My favourite guess at that moment was that he had gone to organise a lift back to New York or some point on the journey for us with the relatives who had come down to the funeral in hired buses. In his absence my mind went back to the church and the singing in it. The melody was all around me now. *Upon the hill, the rising sun...* They were singing in what my preparation for my sojourn into the black South told me was long meter. A note was held like a jetty over water, in which water people and bellows did their thing — jumped over each other, over waves, dived into the waves... *It is the voice.* I slept off again under the jetty with the white waves lashing the greenish white water and the notes in long meter bouncing precariously like mini replicas of Columbus' ships. I woke up to find Reuben sitting on the bed. I had been right, but his walk through the village had imposed a structure other than the one I imagined on to the request of the relatives.

This part of Louisiana is sugar cane. There is relatively little land left for people settlement. Life is therefore close in these enclosures: a man could hear his neighbour at the most intimate of life's acts should he choose to listen. People had come out of these settlements like black ants dressed in white. And nowhere had I seen before such an array of armbands, headgear, banners across the chest, gloves, swords. Styles of dress clustered together — boat shaped hats together, helmets together, aproned groups together and so on, dividing the population accordingly into tribes or classes, each led by a brass band. Banners attached to poles and held by gloved hands separated each group from the other in orderly intervals as they gathered for processing and marched forward with Mammy's remains.

The banners announced the groups to be of the Odd-

Fellows Lodge, the Independent and Protective Order of Tabernacle, Knights and Ladies of Honour in America (this they said was Mammy's lodge), the Most Worshipful Eureka Grand Lodge of Free Accepted Masons and what must surely be its sib — the Most Worshipful Grand Order of the Western States. We had had to scribble surreptiously for there were more than the mind could hold — the Knights of Pythius, Knights and Daughters of Tabor, the Grand Court of Calanthe, the District Grand Household of Ruth.

The funeral had brought down people — relatives I thought — in every kind of conveyance — conveyances to match the distance. There were buses large, buses small, trucks, vans, cars, wagons, bicycles, carts, two seater bikes. Mammy was indeed someone and obviously worthy of study! A fair sample had stayed overnight to enjoy a kinship particularly warm after the death of someone who was slated to go. I couldn't now see them but I could hear them. They were still hanging about although tomorrow was Monday and a work day. It was through and in this group of post funeral mourners that Reuben would have to walk to make whatever arrangements he felt our needs required.

He was back in our house. His smile congratulatory.
–It took nearly all of St Mary to get you out of the church and into this bed.– Reuben doesn't lie. I was embarrassed at having been centre-stage, upstaging even the redoubtable Mammy. Worse was to come. He had gone, as I had thought, to try to get us out on one of the lifts going North but he now felt that I needed to think through certain things though, and had instead asked that the office be informed in my name that Mrs King had died and I was winding up, and had sent some spun tale to his own department to explain his absence for another week. What we needed to think through, he thought, was what was going on with me. His walk through the village had handed him a hypothesis:

Mammy had passed, leaving her soul with me.

It was with great reverence and seriousness, he said, that people were asking after me. They had no problems he said with the shouting and with my violence and my unusual strength. They had seen it all before or had heard of it: it was quite consistent with the transfer of souls. I was being taken on a journey into knowing and was resisting as first timers sometimes do. They hoped my travel was fruitful. I was totally embarrassed. And here was Reuben willing to consider this explanation of the strange behaviour which he described to me as being mine. Something told me to keep my vision of Mammy riding the rainbow to myself as well as my experience with the voices which I had not yet come around to sharing with him.

This is 1936, (remember), Reuben and I have been close for the past three years. We do like each other. Please know this. But life has its calculating and materialistic aspects. From that perspective Reuben is the best thing that has happened to me for a long time and naturally I wish to keep that thing and him. I am an only child. The one and only. Strange for a coloured couple eh! From the little bits those two let out, it seems that my father left me in my mother and went off to Central America where he found that he wanted her company permanently, came back to get her, married her and took her away but not, for whatever reason their child, only few months old. I was left with my grandmother. It is nice to think that she refused to let her grandchild travel at so young an age to some place she didn't know, but there was no way of confirming this. Again from what little they say, I gather that she died in my early infancy.

For as long as I can recall feeling, I have always felt sorrow for those two; seemed to me they had lost the art of babymaking for they had made no one else to warm them, to keep their company and to fill the space between them.

Warmth and companionship were sorely needed. Surely I wouldn't do. I sensed that. Why else were they so rarely with me. With age I expanded this thesis concerning their quasi-barrenness. Work. Work kept them from meeting to make babies. My parents seemed merely to pass each other on their way to work. He was always away — away in the height of his career, as a pullman porter. She too was always away — a nurse's aide. Not a registered nurse as I learnt in my early teens though the kind people called her 'nurse' and had her doing technical jobs for which she had nothing but on-the-job qualifications. I, it seemed to me, was left with the one or the other who happened to be at home and was what joined those two independent circles which hardly touched at what I felt to be baby-making times, the nights.

I was an egg, for those two people held in me the potential for all kinds of things they hadn't done and like an egg if I fell I could break and splatter all over their faces. Somewhere my folks heard of Susan McKinney Steward. There was a picture of her on the wall near to my bed. This particular egg was to be a medical doctor like her. I was bright, able to apply myself. I could have done it. I nearly did it. To create the right environment for my hatching, they said was the reason for their hard, childless work and for their further hard work when I got into medical school. And what does the egg do to those poor souls? Quit medical school after one year. What could they tell their friends and particularly their enemies? "She is pregnant", would make sense. Friends would shake their heads in empathy and say, "You can never put your money on a girl child". Enemies would say, "That's the one natural thing that has happened to those black whites". My woman self would be their shield and buckler and on both sides. But I wasn't pregnant. There wasn't even a man in the woodpile then. Those two had simply produced a being as self-contained as they and as in love with her work — they never admitted that their true passion was for work, — as they. I, their offspring had fallen in love with words and chose to be a word smith. Can a poem take the place of a stethoscope cum office with a brass name plate? That my works and my name — their name — got into *Crisis* and *Opportunity* meant nothing. "'Crisis'? What crisis? These American negroes expect goodies to be put into their laps." "'Opportunity'? One of them burial schemes nuh. How you get mixed up in that?"

They were able to hold their heads up a little bit when I got the job at Columbia and their heads on their shoulders got distinctly steadier when I started bringing Reuben around. That golden boy absolved me. Gave me something to give my luckless parents about whose happiness I did care tremendously. I had only now to marry him and make their joy almost complete and that was a million times more to my liking than driving a needle into somebody's rear. So Reuben is key to my life and I didn't want to jeopardise that relationship. My secret therefore rankled; the burden of it was intolerable and injurious to my social health. Understand?

Reuben is a bright man forever in search of knowledge. He had come all the way from Antwerp to study black folks and had charmed them all, my parents especially, with his quaint accent, his golden brown and his status in the academic world — 'one of the first negroes etc etc'. Better he than me! He had chosen me. His English needed help. I had only recently been made a teaching assistant in writing and he chose to join my class. Because of my race. My golden lover pulled me to him with, among his virtues, his amazing personal history told to me in that very engaging, halting English. A priest, his story went, worried that the closest image to the son of God should be seen by the Congolese natives walking barefooted and half-clothed in their kraal, brought him back to Europe. He was no more than three years old. Many have been our laughing sessions

40

over our joke that he was conceived by immaculate conception in the stomach of said priest who could find no story to hand him concerning his parents, black or white. It was meeting news of DuBois that had this coloured reversing the trend and trekking to America.

Reuben was not just bright and coloured. He was of the German school of Sociology. Had traipzed around and been taught by the greats — Weise, Stein, the lot, been field assistant to one and been well thought of by them. German Sociology was in, so Reuben had a place in America. It was not Sociology though, but his status and the fact that he was golden, and neither white nor black-black and too foreign to have disreputable and embarrassing relatives, that made my parents willing to accept his doctorate-to-be as a good trade off for my stethoscope and brass name plate. With me it was the way his mind worked. I loved that and that was what trapped me now. I was the black soul that Reuben studied most closely. He knew what he was doing then when after a day made unpleasant by my refusal to share things he suspected I was hiding and by my refusal to do anything but laugh at the explanation of my behaviour that originated from St Mary's natives and which Reuben wanted me to swallow, he said in his guttural:

–How unfortunate when we realise that we are nothing more than the people!– This was meant to tell me that I was a hypocrite, pretending to take race seriously, pretending to take the field's sense of itself seriously but balking when that explanation was applied to my own behaviour; that for all my race consciousness I was making a distinction between myself and the people around me and who was I.

Well who was he? I had a vested interest in Reuben's person but that in no way stopped me from defending myself. Who was he! I spoke in anger but there was truth in my position. I knew my parents. I had them to protect. Was I to embarrass them further by becoming some hoodoo woman to satisfy his search for the exotic? He was nobody's business, his priest father having died. He had nobody to be ashamed of him. And the bilge about social difference, there were social differences. He only didn't recognise them because (a) he was foreign (b) he was so set on finding himself in the new world of Negroes that if he was told that coloureds barked, he would gladly bark and in any case why the USA? Why not the Congo? Let them tell him there to eat human flesh and see if he would do it.

Whether it is his lack of facility with the language or his personality, I cannot say, but Reuben's facial muscles do have the oddest way of saying contradictory things all at once. So with his eyes still bold-faced and critical, his muscles and his voice said in the most penitent manner, sorrowful and isolated: "They even took me to Ceylon but not there" — so much so that I felt sorry for him, the little boy who had been stolen from Congo drums and planted in the silent North and the man wandering in search of a connection. So sorry, that I sought to comfort them. One thing led to another and another to another much to the delight of the no-longer-sweet-smelling sheets. They clapped their hands for joy.

If there was something to win I must have won it because next morning we started packing. We hadn't had much time to discuss my work and in any case I had not wanted to talk about the voices — how do you tell someone that you have been in unspoken conversation with others visible and invisible? — so I had before shrugged off all his questions verbal and non-verbal. Now as we packed we talked. I had said and held that I had got nothing worthwhile from Mammy. I did say Reuben is a scholar! Under his questioning, I realised that in cross-examining me about my past, Mammy had given me information on her own past. We thought we'd listen to this before packing up the instrument and working on the closing report to be

42

submitted to my director. Reuben ofcourse scolded me for not listening to the reel before. This was rhetorical scolding because he knew the reason why and appreciated it. "How come so much of the spool is used if there was so little conversation?" That was easy to answer. "I have my style of data collection. Collect the dog's bark, the wind whispering and collect non-verbal expressions." "But there is a lot of verbal activity on this tape", he said. That was news to me and when I listened I heard Mammy's voice in more places than I had known her to speak. "The flirt" I said, "She had that lad operate the machine and answered my questions for me." Reuben was amazed that I had left the machine with her but I could explain that. What I could no how explain was what was on the reel. You have heard it. Nobody needed to tell me that I had a lot of thinking to do and I had to do it right there.

Some words control large spaces. They sit over large holes. These holes might be dungeons with hairy half humans living in them. Then again they may be underground worlds with railway lines taking trains and neatly dressed people here and there. I met some of these words at my mother's church — the Episcopalian church. "Fear not", said he, "For might dread had seized their troubled hearts." 'Dread' is one of these words. "Before Jehovah's aweful throne, ye nations bow... " 'Aweful' was another and 'confound' another. Weekly they prayed, "Never let me be confounded". These words — 'dread', 'aweful', 'confounded' — were on name plates in any path I had to tread, rather like the iron grates over a city's sewage. These iron grates are set in concrete and are predictable more or less. You will find them at the side of the road near the curb. The sidewalk is elevated; the road cambers, so that it is on the rare occasion that you need to walk on them. My grates were structurally different. In fact they weren't grates at all. They were name plates and could appear anywhere on the street or the side walk. They belonged to another civilisation and the modern day had not unearthed the key to their location. They were rather like the flaps on a letter box. Made of tin or enamel. And set in tin or enamel. And these you know can corrode — vide the constant need for the soldering man.

I lived in fear that one day I would step on one of those rotten corroded words and go hurtling down into nowhere. Perhaps my body in the long drop would veer to the right or to the left and I'd be stuck crossways like rainstorm. Today those three name plates in their most rotten and corroded existence came together. We fell down, down, down. We were lucky. There was a lot of space so no reason to be stuck. And the fall was fairly smooth. Perhaps because we were holding hands. And it was a bed of leaves on which we fell. Scented, pressed, thin, velvety leaves. They made hardly a sound when our bodies connected with them. That was one plus for the situation. Thanks to that fall I will never be afraid of falling again, I thought then.

After we had learnt that the reel was full, not of silences but of words, not of someone like Jack Johnson meddling or playing tricks or of Mammy reeling out her life story as a parting gift to a well-favoured me, but of conversations between two women, one of them Mammy, with interjections from me in words I didn't know, we immediately forwarded the spool and listened from Lowly's song right through to the end. We fell off the end of that reel right through those word holes. In awe and dread and totally confounded, we lay together on the narrow still-scented bed in silence.

"Do I need to see a psychiatrist?", I had asked aloud of myself. You know Reuben's reply based on inadequate information.

I knew things Reuben did not know. I knew that I had heard voices; that my mind had been spoken aloud while the recording machine was on; I knew that I had heard myself say things in my head that I couldn't know and ofcourse I had seen Mammy's ascension. As I recovered from the numbness of the fall and felt reason putting these experiences together with the content of the reel, I realised that only I knew all these things and therewith sensed the existence of another and larger rotten name plate on my side of the bed. This time round I would be falling by myself. I wasn't sure that I could manage that. The name-plate on my side of the bed had twin words on it, again from my mother's church service. They were 'sore' and 'distress'. The connection between the content of the reel and my own unrevealed experiences was frightening. 'Sore distress' was about to pluck me from Reuben's side and swallow me. I felt another name plate about to give way under me. This time it was a sentence from my mother's psalter. They used to say it in that sing-song they call chanting — "The Lord shall have them in derision". Isolation locked eyes with me and threatened, with staged laughter echoing all around, to take me off by myself to the dreadful, aweful, confounding basement of this phenomenon which had so boldy left its portrait upon the people's recording machine.

I must have jumped at the imminent threat for Reuben turned to me with a question on his face. In half an hour he knew all that I knew.

—It makes sense— is all that he said. Then to himself,

—Was that the ring shout?— And to me,

—As you writhed and shouted, they formed a circle around you and did a kind of shoe patter accompanied by deep grunts. It was monotonous; the beat didn't change. That calmed you into a faint. It was only after that that we were able to lift you—

—Reuben, why hadn't you told me that before?— I asked, as if I could have dealt with the knowledge then.

45

−So many things are new to me. Actuality does not always accord with the literature. The statistical norm... − a language problem! Reuben used to have tremendous problems with expressing himself informally. I broke in:

−If for instance this is the ring shout, it is not the classic case− But the function certainly was the same. I had been officially entered. I was going to be, if I was not already, a vessel, a horse, somebody's talking drum.

−Do I need a psychiatrist?− I put the question directly to him this time. He was even more sure that this was something we had to keep to ourselves.

−Although altogether− another of his favourite English phrases placed for style rather than meaning I remember −there are different yet logical systems of knowledge and your director knows that, yet I don't think that he is ready for this.−

* * *

A man and a woman together for hours in a darkened cottage must have signified for some of the people living around this foreign couple, an active honeymoon. The truth was otherwise. We spent the whole night lying together in silence. We didn't work; we didn't eat; didn't go to the bath-house; didn't light the lamps; didn't think of continuing with our packing; didn't discuss an alternate course; didn't anything. Tired and listless in the morning, we told ourselves that something had to be done and left it there. Thank God for chores. They told us what to do, so we went to buy bread. There were no eggs. We went to get eggs. Lunch time was approaching. Soup would be good. We went to get vegetables. We hadn't moved the recording machine. We hadn't touched it. With night and the closing of windows, space becomes smaller and articles of furniture in the house more distinguishable. Our night was a moonlight night. One

46

of those celebrated in Southern songs... "Shine on, shine on harvest moon". The moon came right through the slat windows and spotlighted the machine. We could not escape its presence.

I hadn't been in my little St Mary village for long. My business had been to get in touch with, to try to know and to machine record, the life of Mrs Sue Ann King and I had focused on her. There are others like me working throughout the nation. I don't know how they were chosen. In my case Prof. introduced himself to me as one of the directors of this nation-wide project, told me he knew of me and felt I was what he was looking for to go down into Louisiana. He told me I'd be given leave from my teaching assistantship, be made a fellow in Anthropology for the duration of the project and that I would be expected to make myself available for pre-field training. Which wasn't much. The most challenging part was handling a recording machine. At the end of it, I was given a brief bio. of Mrs King. 'A most original story-teller' is all that stood out. I could have been given more information if I had pressed him, I think, but it was my feeling that anything more got through him might prejudice me and I wanted the excitement of going into the field fresh and raw to follow what trails I felt like following. I therefore didn't probe. I just packed my suitcase and headed for Louisiana. The spareness of my knowledge about my St Mary district, then, is nobody's fault but mine. Not a fault really, just a programme that backfired leaving me a total stranger in my setting.

I had been quite neighbourly for the fortnight or so that I had been there. I had smiled, entered light conversation, bought food, been done favours to and returned favours but I hadn't taken the people around me very seriously. Afterall it was Mammy on whom I was to focus and my director had assured me that the field had been prepared; those who

47

needed to be informed of my presence had been so informed and so on. Now that Mammy was no longer in the flesh, there was a change. The cross on the female sign had gone, leaving the circle and me a part of this round for as long as I stayed in St Mary. And I knew so little of thesociology of the place! I knew Mrs Forbes. I knew her to be a jittery woman who had some skills in nursing — the doctor had thought she could have given Mammy her injections — but I couldn't even begin to imagine where Mrs Forbes had trained or where for that matter had the doctor trained. Did they have to leave the South to train? I knew not. Who were the high-statused in this settlement of sugar cane workers? How do you identify them? To whom must I defer?

Coming into the village on my first day and in my coming and going to and from Franklin to meet and collect Reuben, I had seen stores, their ambiance quite different from the little rural Harlem in which I lived. This was the white part of the area. I had no problems recognising it and though I did feel some fear as I passed by, it was relatively little since I knew that my director had surely prepared the likes of those for my entry into their South, into the part of the village in which they did not live. I didn't spend much mental energy on them. I was only going to be around for about a month, wasn't I? Now they began to have faces in my mind. What was their relationship to the village. Who was big Massa? What was his name? I didn't even know that.

November was fully here and with it the chill but Reuben and I were spending a lot of time outside. By common unspoken consensus we had decided to snob our odd room mate. Being outside drew us into the sociology: we were invited into people's houses. Questions about social structure whirled in my head; questions about politics, global and otherwise whirled in the heads of our hosts. Their interest in me was peripheral. I was only one of theirs gone North and everybody and his wife had people 'up there'. Moreover I sensed a kind of impatience with me. I felt it had to do with me as a woman but couldn't figure out what was the precise problem. Did it matter that I was sharing my life with a man who hadn't married me? How would they know about our marital status anyhow? Was there some bow or salaam that the female part of the duo ought to perform and I had not so done? Or did they think me out of order to be walking out with this man when I should be cleaning the house or doing some other female chore? Or were they waiting for me to give them some message from Mammy to fulfill their sense of me as the possessed? What would that be anyhow? Well there was nothing to tell or that I wished to tell, so if the discomfort were to disappear, it would have to find some other route. Gender was the pre-determined one as it happened. It was right there in the traditional division of labour that the change came.

Reuben helped me with the preparation of our meals but with our instability — not knowing when we would leave, not even knowing what would make us leave, we took to buying our food when we needed to eat. A major part of meal preparation therefore was going to the store. Reuben did this and with the passing days came to be in charge of our foreign relations. I did the tidying of the little cottage: internal affairs fell into my portfolio. This meant less interaction with the folk and less discomfort for them for they saw me less. It also meant that I couldn't avoid dusting the recording machine. I found myself talking to it: "Yes, you there, I see you and I am going to dust you. Think you are going to stop me from tidying this house, you blinking black box?" Then I'd flog/dust the machine with the rag held long. It was part of our family ritual now when Reuben came in, for me to relate the nature of my contact with the machine. I would lay down a line and we would go on adding to what had taken place and building on to it fantastic stories that had us cracking our sides. He might begin a conversation with, "How were the ladies this morning?" I might reply, "Today I flogged them with the dusting cloth; tomorrow I will pick up their whole house and put them over that corner." On his return from one of his many sallies, he might ask, "Have you dispossessed the ladies as yet?" And that would be a bigger and deeper set of laughs. "Dead weight", I might say, "I couldn't get them to budge."

Without planning it, we were demystifying the poor old thing. It was this process that finally led me to opening the recording machine gently and reverently as if I was cleaning my baby daughter's private region. I listened, back-tracked, listened and wrote. The cross was back on the circle and me alone with the sisters for Reuben was usually out roving... until the day he came in and heard his name. What he heard was no new news. He had heard his name the first day we played the reel through. No new news. Just a new Reuben.

That first morning with the box, I had pulled it tentatively towards me. Having moved it, I began to feel like a lover pulling his love to him and asking why. A why they both understood in all its nuances. "Why did you forsake me?", "Why did you go off with another?", "Why wouldn't you let me in?", "Why did you scratch me?", "Why can't you like my mother?", "Why did you lock me out of our pregnancy?", "Why will you not speak eh?", "Why are you now so cold with me?", "Why?". I felt a softness in that box, the-about-to-cry phase and tell-all phase and I could sense the reconciliation coming. I, the lover, pressed on to opening and to fingering, to locating the essentials, the paper and pencil and to getting ready for the profound intimacy.

I depressed the button. With that touch my head grew large, suffused by my liquified body. "Let go", I heard myself say to myself. I let go and was all ears. I listened. I heard the song of the first lady. I back-tracked and back-tracked until the words were clear. Truly the lady was no singer. But whate'er the melody the tune and the lyrics were unmistakenly familiar. That last time I had heard them I had collapsed. That was something else to think of — the collapse. But let me leave me out of this and get the obvious down on paper, I commanded myself. *Upon the hill, the rising sun. It is the voice that calls me home.* They had sung that at Mammy's funeral. And according to this lady it was sung at her funeral which had taken place somewhere else. That was extraordinary. I would have to meditate on that.

There were words in the narrative that I didn't know. Couldn't even hear because they were so unfamiliar. I'd leave them and get back to them when other and more accessible things were clear. "Birds dressed in white", "banners", "band". In that clearing called the village surrounded as it was by cane, such a gathering of black people, dressed in white, did look like a multitude of white birds in some African forest. The banners held aloft were the plumage of the turkey, the guinea hen. This lady was indeed describing a funeral, the larger version of which I had experienced. What she described was the small photo; Mammy's funeral was the enlargement of the self-same photo.

"Ah who sey Sammy dead", I heard myself say just about the same time as my very weak voice on reel whispered it. So this was somehow about the dead. Two different women. Two different places. Two different times. Buried in similar rites. Was that it? So why was I there? Why was I in their conversation and how and why was I moved in this my other self — I obviously had two — to say this, *"Ah who sey Sammy dead?"* No answer came. Only another seepage from an experience I hadn't realised had had such an impact on me,

–Death where is they sting
Grave where is thy victory?–

From my mother's episcopalianism.

That was a whole week. Week 1, and with the back-tracking to find the right place, listening, back-tracking, writing, revising, I was drained, but tall. I had entered. I had listened, been with them and hadn't collapsed. I was positively preening. I had eaten that little bit of cake, squeezed through, drunk just the right amount of that liquid, grown to their size, stabilised myself and was hobnobbing on equal terms! I had arrived. Passed through my rite of passage with flying colours. I had broken through that membrane and was in, ready and willing to be and see something else. Transform, change, focus Transform, change. I was a woman among women. This is my report upon reflection and upon guided reflection through the years.

Afternoons I turned myself into Reuben's woman. Here he was more often than not, jabbering away in his gutterals like somebody's lisp-tongued boy, soup or whatever, flying from his lunch-time mouth. He had found that little capillary that was to take him right back to the tall oak he was trying to find in his Congo, in the heart of Africa. His Sociology had paid off afterall. Reuben had found black men. Startling! Yes. But not for a chap who had been brought up seeing only whites. Only he in that European community perceived the true scope of his difference from them. For them he was simply far left, very far left on the people continuum and the thing about people was that they were of varying shades of pink and white. For him though there was a whole other world under his isolated spot on that continuum. He wanted to fathom it. He wanted to put his measuring rod down that hole and push his hooks down, down and dig until he found that world. The occasional smell wafted up. From the little tentative holes he could make he sensed DuBois and followed that scent until it took him to America.

The very brightness that had paid Reuben's passage here led him into what he had left behind. The academy was white but here in the United States of America he could at least hear, see and, having found me, touch blackness. In St Mary, Louisiana, he was wallowing in it. Never before in his thirty years had he been part of the majority. So he was strutting, strumming, learning to jazz and getting acquainted with the blues. Not that he was a total stranger to these two latter, for he had met them in Europe and had ferretted out every music making spot there was in New York. But these products there were processed. In this Louisiana canefield sounds and styles were coming hot out of the oven. He was feeling them in the making, was there at their conception. The man was being made anew.

Out of Eden

My mother's church had a stained glass window with a thorn-headed picture of Jesus the Christ, his head slightly leaned to one side, his arms open and his fingers delicately cocked reminding me somehow of the proper way of drinking tea. You could see his heart — it was heart shaped and had, I think, a dart going through it. At his feet in halos were women, the Marys I presumed. The picture was a mosaic, like a jigsaw puzzle. Someone must have painted it on glass, broken it into pieces of uneven sizes then stuck the parts together in that large window sited over the altar. How did they do this and why? The picture responded to light, so that bits of it or the whole were only visible as it was directed towards them. There was no street lamp or beacon close by, revelation had to depend on God's natural light. In winter therefore, there was hardly more of this picture to be seen than the raised lines in the mosaic where the parts were joined. With the coming of the sun and the summer, the whole picture was there and for a considerable time.

The services my mother attended began at six am. She had no choice but to take me with her, my father being unavailable to us at those times, he having just returned from somewhere and needing his sleep and not the bother of his daughter, his only child. It was more often than not dark then and no picture to be seen for the whole hour and a half at that church but as the days grew longer I could watch the parts individually revealing themselves and I'd leave the church with the whole picture in my head.

The stained glass window vied with the over-shirts of the processing men for my attention. My mother fancied the aisle and we were always early enough to sit close by it, so

I did have a good view not only of the stained glass window but also of the men walking slowly and reverently behind each other and behind the man who carried the cross. Those over-shirts bothered me. Who did that delicate embroidery? It had to be a woman. Not my mother; she didn't have the time though she could have had the skill. I do not know. I ruled her out and searched the napes of the necks of those sitting before us and the faces of those returning from communion, for that angel. Had I got into the church society I might have been able to identify her but I wasn't confirmed — I dropped out of church-going before I entered high school.

This church, my mother's church, was called by those around us the West Indian church and West Indians were called King George's negroes. They were a funny lot. They kept themselves away from others on their blocks and formed their own clubs and societies, yet in these groups they seemed as apart from each other as they were from those outside them. You would think for instance that having segregated themselves from their neighbours and from America in general, they would be together glorifying their islands and swopping tidbits about home, but this was not so. True, there was talk of how-we-did-it-back-home when they found something wrong with their neighbour's behaviour but getting some details on how 'they did it back home', was as difficult for me and as painful for them as pulling teeth.

Each was a history book, separate, zippered and pad-locked. Some like my own parents had even thrown away their keys! I didn't like being called King George's negro — I didn't even know in any sensible who King George was and what he had to do with me. I most certainly didn't like being seen as different, being consequently kept isolated and that without some clear portrait of my distinguishing features, so the West Indian church, the church of King George's negroes couldn't hold me. My parents didn't know why. I guess they thought that I thought that full participation in church might lessen my studying time and I was doing well. They pardoned my rebellion.

I didn't know that more was happening for me at my mother's church than my meditation on the stained glass window and the men's over-shirts but there obviously was. Look at how quickly I responded to Mammy's reference to the temptations! And here now I want to talk about sugar cane and find myself pulling from that past and saying: "For I thy God am a jealous god." Cane is a jealous god. It needs every ounce of energy of every man, woman and child. This is especially so in November going on to December, the time when we were there. This is reaping season and every stalk must be in before the winter sets in. I was in my cottage with the venerable sisters and as far as the public could see, distracting no one. All concerned were now, I imagined, happy with me. I certainly was happy.

Reuben was out of doors more often than not, hanging around, hoping to talk to new friends in their dinner break or in their after work time, intent on perfecting that chord or making sure that he did get the meaning behind those lyrics. How distracting! People would be thinking about the time they would be having with him later, rather than thinking about sugar cane. Had I thought through the matter sufficiently, I might have seen the problem and been able to avert it but as I have said, I had paid little attention to the sociology and my late and desultory attempts seemed unwelcome in the village. I had in any case come to be with one woman. The one woman had turned into two and here was I now totally taken up by them and the machine through which they communicated with me.

Week 2. Mammy is speaking. Reuben was right; she has given information about herself. Mammy did marry Silas and had children by him. By him — not so sure. He had been to some war, brought back disease which affected the whole family and died leaving her to carry on. She was epileptic and went away from time to time as I had seen her do and though she hoped that these attacks and her other maladies would take her to her final rest, was always drawn back by the intervention of some kind or needy other. I was beginning to see the character. A sort of matriarch. I was beginning to see her physical self as a young woman — the same Mammy I saw on the rainbow. Fat head of hair. Does one become rejuvenated after death? Does the spirit choose to return in its favourite physical form? Mammy and her friend did like her fat head of hair.

Somewhere I have heard that dead friends of the dying come to carry them home — "Get those old water-logged feet to swing off the ground and... " It appeared that Mammy had been making her final exit just about the time I started interviewing her and that her friend Lowly — What a name! — had come to accompany her home. What was on the reel so far, if that was the case, was a recording of what took place during this visit. But there was a hitch. Lowly says: "And this thanksgiving" meaning her own funeral some years before, and Mammy says "How was I ... to sail cross the sea... ?" Lowly must then, some years ago have invited her to her funeral, or invited her to die and join her. What a thought! They would have to have been able to communicate with each other telepathically not only across space as I knew it but from terrestial to extra terrestial. When and how did Lowly's speech get on the recording machine if she had spoken in the past when it was not there? Mammy must have recalled her. Mammy must have recalled her : "And I had heard you that time". Yes. Mammy on her way to the other world recalled that event and so powerfully that it was recorded on the machine. Or did the machine pull it from her, from her friend and from me? That meditation later. Mammy's recall was not the end of Lowly. She was there continually after and in the present. So was I. What was I doing there? At one level the question was superfluous: I was there because the director chose to send me there. But what about the other levels?

Mammy had thought I was her old friend come in the flesh to take her home. That was an ordinary enough mistake and she soon got that straight. "Two women sire another!", Lowly had teased by way of explanation. She was saying, there is a bond but we are three separate people. I stepped back a bit to ask myself what was my head into — the anthropology of the dead? Celestial ethnography? Crazy. I turned myself back with that break to thinking about the subject I had been paid to come to Louisiana to study. Mammy. Mammy had married Silas — lived with? — certainly felt responsible for Silas; had a child perhaps by him. Did I meet any child of hers at the funeral? Must check about children. She and her friend Lowly had worked in some place where there had been a victrola. Mammy was considerably older and was to her a self-appointed guardian. "Green gal from the islands." Her friend was from the West Indies. Mammy herself was from the South, right here and had fled unwillingly it seems to the North. They both worked in the kitchen of what would be a rooming house in which this Silas was a paying guest.

Odd. It was Lowly who used to visit his room but it was Mammy who married him/settled with him. Visiting the guests was unacceptable for maids. Fair enough. Punishment was being banished to the "downtown, no-count kitchen". This proprietor was not struggling: she had two establishments. This was a woman and in Chicago. Not bad for a woman. Why did Mammy flee the South? End of week 2.

An analytical scheme was developing as I was transcribing. When I had the contents of the reel on paper I would look at Mammy's personal history, at her relationship with her friend — that would be the academic part — then for my own curiosity, I would look at their perception of me, the interviewer. What did they really mean by "This is the horse will you ride"? Could it mean what I thought it meant? I resembled them; they looked like me... but let discipline prevail. I would deal with that when its time comes.

Week 3. Fairly straightforward. My ears had become accustomed. There were no new players so all I had to do was to concentrate on hearing the words. "Perseus", "Andromeda" and so forth. Mammy's friend was quite well-read. The place they met was Chicago. Mammy's little friend was from Jamaica and Mammy had thought she was pregnant by Silas. This mistake lead them to a more equal friendship. Nothing new in Mammy's history except perhaps for her great capacity for concealing excitement. She was phlegmatic, her friend was sanguine. It was as if they were two halves of an orb. They were as amazed as I was by the wholeness which they made — Mammy in her stony way, her friend in her volatile way.

The set of coincidences which drew them into a bracket, hit the sisters equally but was manifested in distinctly different ways. How remarkable though — relatives of the same name, born and bred in areas of the same name and after this, buried in the same way. There is no clear information on the shape that this sense of their oneness took in their life time though the existence of Silas does indicate a shared chord, and certainly on the reel there is the suggestion that a physical orb had been transformed into a spiritual one which crossed the seas and earth and heaven and held in Mammy's translation the hope of a more productive bonding and subsequent action.

Week 4 was difficult. A great deal of backing and forthing preceded transcription, so Reuben kept hearing his name at the end of one of my morning sessions. He came in as I was trying to patch words together and make sense of the section that seemed to deal so much with me. "Golden boy", "Chimboraza". I kept going back and forth. "Golden boy", "Reuben". He came in in quiet excitement. "This is it." "What is 'it'?" I asked. "This is where I belong." I must have been very far from this guy over the past weeks, I thought, for me to see this announcement as so out of line. The transition from investigator to aspiring resident had quite escaped me though I was aware that his research was becoming more subjective than was good science. But what did it matter? He was holidaying. "What's this about?" I asked. "I have found my family", was the bald reply. I said nothing. His response to this discovery was to spend more time with me. Strange.

Week 5. I continued to transcribe and to draft conceptual schemes in my head. Reuben was satisfied to stay home and do the fair copy of the transcriptions as I passed my pages to him. Strange. "Isn't it clear?" he asked me after a couple days into faircopying, aware that I was too non-plussed by his transformation to ask sensible questions. I shook my head. It wasn't. All his sense of journey's end did bring into my little light was another brand of opaqueness. Was he serious about settling in St Mary, Louisiana, or was the whole South the home he found? I knew he did not mean the North. So what about the job? His career? What was he saying about our future and ofcourse my parents' hopes? How did he intend to make a living? These issues threatened to come between me and the little rays of understanding that were beginning to peep through this odd happening. So I held my head stubbornly down and pressed on with my work. The shared transcript had to stand in for interest, concern, empathy, all those things a friend should feel for another who has just made a momentous decision. My head was just too tired. Let it be said for me though, that I kept our weekend games of german whist going and even managed to win some.

Week 6. I felt I had all the words down. Analysis. I had got no further with Mammy's history. Let me scour the reel again for any escaped gem. On separate pieces of paper list names of people mentioned, list names of places mentioned, list cultural items, then add data as found. This was my analytical frame, so I had sheets of paper headed Lowly, Ezekiel, Silas, Donna Claire, the mistress, Ramrod Grant and ofcourse Sue Ann Grant-King. This was file 1. File 2 had ofcourse Louisiana, St Mary (Jamaica), St Mary, Louisiana (USA), Chicago. Chicago Southside. In file 3 were sheets headed Dinkie mini, john-crow-blow-nose, the bannered groups by name, shepherd, rag-songs, victrola, units — "units set up", she had said — Arkansas devilment, coon can, longshoreman's strike. The only date given me was the earthquake (Jamaica) 1907. I would rinse and rinse until everything was down, then with my one little date I would try the historical reconstruction of the life of Mrs Sue Ann Grant-King. A voice said, "To what avail" but I ignored it.

Then me. File 4. I would write down all that I had said. I would note the points at which I entered; I would write out all that was said about me… a,b,c. 'a' was short. I had just kept saying, *"Ah who sey Sammy dead"*. I spoke to Mammy — nothing of consequence — greetings, responses to her question. Comments which I had made in my head were there; my intentions concerning Reuben were there. If they were news to him, it was fully time he should know of them. No, that didn't bother me. It no longer even bothered me that I was selected by them for some job. The sense of imposition had been annoying… "Get back here!", I had to tell myself. My thoughts had gone way out of the schedule laid down in my scheme and now I was preoccupied out of turn by file 4 and transfixed by the nature of my place in the triangle and in particular by the fact that the sisters possessed a history of me of which I had just the faintest glimpse, a history so personal and tucked away — flying and the old lady.

It was never as clear for me as they presented it. In my dreams there was this accordion-type bellows of leather on which I floated. The feeling of exhilaration, of seeing all/ knowing all was there and suddenly deflation was there, and accompanying it, a feeling of confusion, absence, depression. The concreteness and the instancing which they presented was never there for me. But it all made sense after I had read and absorbed their comments. The things they mentioned were indeed my experience but something blocked me from seeing more than the leather. That leather was of course the beauty, firmness, dignified aging of the old lady. I do love leather. That was the old lady, my Granny. I yearned to know more of that story and set myself the task of listening to the sisters again and again contrary to my schedule, until I could capture in all its dimensions the story of my grandmother and me. Big white feet further rearranged my schedule.

It was cold; the doors were shut. They knocked; I opened the door. They were quite polite to me. "We know why you are here, though we reckoned you'd be gone what with the old lady dead. But there be no call for no Reuben Cole to be back here." Reuben was at the table writing. He had looked up at the knock and gone back to his work when I answered the door and, smelling danger, must have looked up again so that the threatening eyes made four with his. "He's my friend" I said. As if I had not spoken, the eyes and the shoes on my doorstep continued, "We kicked you out of here ten years before. Get out and stay out." My mouth was wide open. Was this another apartment in the surrealistic world into which the recording machine had plummeted me? Before I could catch my breath he had left, this my first male white contact in the South. Reuben's

65

"didn't I tell you", didn't help.

Didn't he tell me what? That he 'had been here before'. "This is the South, Reuben, and that was a white man. This is not a... " and I nearly said 'joke'. That I figured would have had us laughing as we have done so many times over Reuben's inability to pronounce that word, and would have detracted from the seriousness of the matter so I rephrased: "This is a serious matter". I could have saved my breath for he looked seriously at me and said "No yoke" with the normal result. After I had recovered I continued, "Reuben you were not here ten years ago, so what is this about?" Then the story came out as Southern as 'polly-wolly-doodle-all-the day'. That the conclusions drawn by Reuben's new black friends so closely resembled that of the eyes and the shoes that had just left my doorstep, was more than remarkable. Reuben too was accepting this interpretation of the situation. I know Reuben and know that he needed to feel that he had at last found people who had a picture of himself to give him and that he felt this so deeply that he would do mental gymnastics in this service. I did not know the psyche of the South, black or white so this mutual suspension of reason floored me.

The explanation, the setting and the story, sing polly wolly doodle all the day. The village had with one accord accepted Reuben. I have before mentioned that there was something about me which irritated them. I was to learn that it was not me personally that was the irritant. They wanted me out of the way, yes, but not because of me. They wanted me out of the way so that they could be with Reuben. I was now understanding that he represented something pleasant in their common past. They hugged this feeling of pleasure closely to themselves, refusing to submit its referent to careful analysis. Someone decided to give voice — and the crazy South took shape for me — "You sure you ain't been here before?" "He your brother?". To cut a long story short, a Reuben Cole — spelt C-O-L-E-, the English version — had been there ten or so years ago. He had been trying to organise them into a union and had been booted out of the area by the owners and their lackeys. The man was white. Reuben is not. Lightly pigmented, yes and there were advantages at home in our northern existence, in being taken by the others, as was reasonable given his name and his accent, for a European Jew, but our people never made this mistake. "I am Reuben Kohl", Reuben must have told that one. Not being there but knowing Reuben, I surmise that he placed the accent wrongly, putting it on 'I am' rather than on 'Kohl'. A general nodding of heads must have followed throughout the village... Reuben Cole is here again, a whiteman grown younger and metamorphosed into a half-breed to continue his work. Man so brave! Damn smart fellow that! They just couldn't keep him out! The resulting adulation and expectation of action kept Reuben home with me. This golden boy, by-passing the fact of a mistaken identity, had reached a place called 'Destiny'. The sound of my strange reel continuously saying "Reuben", as I tried to get the words down correctly, added to his sense of being chosen. Reuben was at home with me, going through my transcript in the hope that it would stimulate in him some thinking that would lend concrete shape to a decision he felt he was called to make.

It had seemed odd to me that the eyes and the shoes had not called Reuben 'boy'. I had vaguely wondered about that. Literature exaggerates. It could be, the contradictory thought ran through my mind, that this linguistic status marker is less used than the literature makes us believe. What I realised after, is that the eyes and shoes on my doorstep saw a white man. They too and others in their caste, for they were only the messengers, had stripped my boy of his golden colour, his wiry hair and his youth and made him into that long gone union organiser whom I was quite sure was balding and wrinkled by now if not rotting in some grave. I did not know what to do with this communal levitation of the senses. It was too much to ask a person to deal with her own private flight from reality as well as this public one, all in the same month. All I could do was perspire and that I did profusely in that little plastered cottage, warmed only by a few embers left over in my coal pot and by my oil lamp.

Reuben watched me break into a sweat on his behalf and would not budge. He was not going to leave, was his contribution to the resolution of the dilemma. To rile me further he would even add in parenthesis "this time". Reasoning didn't help: "You know the kind of visa you have; you can only work with Columbia." "I will not leave" was the refrain. "I will not leave another time." "You cannot go back to Europe. Your betters are losing their jobs for their politics as much as their race. Does Hitler love you more than they, more than he loves Jesse Owens?" "I will not leave." "You will have to find somewhere else to go." He would not budge. It is in times like these that one knows one's friends. The venerable sisters had said that they would use their knees to break my fall. They did.

* * *

My mother was a tall lady. More accurately she looked like a tall lady. She held her head erect, swivelling it right or left only when she needed to see what the world was doing and these were rare occasions. I don't suppose she even knew that she was one of King George's negroes or that our neighbours did not love us. How could she know that? Her ears and eyes are in her head and her head was way above that of her neighbours. I know that nobody but my father could have put a seed in this woman and in addition abandon her if only for months. She was not taller than he but she looked so. His shoulders were rolled, so that his head didn't go straight up in the air like hers; it tended to project into the future like that of pleistocene man or earlier. My father looked like an inventor in the process of inventing. He walked in a dream in the road intensely preoccupied with measuring the distance as if his computation was key to world peace or as if he traversed one long shaky corridor to the end of which he had to carry a tray balanced on the palm of his right hand and on which lay the precious potion which would placate the gorgon and save the world. Nobody felt connected to him enough to say " Yea" or "Nay" as he passed along, shoulders rolled, head forward, concentrating on balancing his tray or measuring the distance.

That he was away so often and really didn't know what was going on did nothing to temper this genetic other worldliness. I could see this man absent-mindedly inventing me and just as absent-mindedly walking away from his invention to work on another world mending device while my mother continued to hold her head aloft. In those days when I had to imagine cause and effect, I supposed that it would have to be in my early inter-uterine days that he left us, before my mother's womb could make connection with that erect head for I couldn't imagine my mother knowing of her pregnancy and not casually tapping him on the shoulder and reminding him that he had forgotten something. I confirmed this in one of my earliest efforts at archival research. I found their marriage certificate. His address was given as Colon and hers, Windsor Castle, St Mary, Jamaica. The marriage took place about six months before my birth. It was about three months after the event then and perhaps as many months after his departure that the womb's signals reached my mother's head, that she stood on her hill, cast her head in the direction of Colon, focussed her eyes, signalled to him that something was amiss and pulled him back to correct it. The lady had poise, presence and a commanding air. She was more often than not in her nurse's uniform — white dress, white shoes, white cap. With this image of the nurse etched on my consciousness, I had assessed Mrs Forbes negatively.

While my mother, even after I had humiliated her, was an egret, stalking through snow, sleet and the heat of the summer street, Mrs Forbes was a round tick hiding in some animal's hair, to be lifted out eventually by that cleaning bird's beak. At Mammy's pre-death bed she had hovered in the back and left me in charge and had run off for help when according to the doctor she ought to have been able to manage the situation. Well, here was Mrs Forbes standing on my doorstep. Her little black round face in the heavy scarf meant to keep the cold out, was a tick in a dog's hair. Like the tick, her feet were invisible. Little and plump, her jutting hips masked her feet. Tonight they were more invisible as she wore a long coat. Mrs Forbes had never visited me. It wasn't the habit of the village to drop in on me, but Mrs Forbes and I had worked together in a sense, so I half expected that she more than anyone else would feel able to intrude especially after my behaviour in the church. I was not by any means unhappy about her no-show. It is just that a show would not have surprised me. Anyhow here was Mrs Forbes now, at the most psychologically inconvenient time. I was just not getting through to Reuben. I suppose he was not getting through to me either. We were both very aware that the village had stopped its breath, waiting for action from us before it could spring into life again. This made me tense. And here was this boneless old lady crawling into my disquiet. Step on her and she would flatten into a sack with murky dark red blood all around it.

Mrs Forbes is so inept, it is difficult not to put your hand under her elbow and settle her. She is the quintessential patient. Mammy must have loved having this wimp around. "Poor Forbes. She wouldn't know." Mammy needed to have 'poor Forbes' around so she could think even in her physical demise, 'poor somebody'. It was not immediately clear to me where I would put 'poor Forbes' to sit. Anyone who had ever visited us had either sat on the steps or just leaned against the wall, hands in the pockets and one foot pressing against the wall. Hardly Mrs Forbes' style and at night and in the cold. Reuben had been lying on the bed. I had been sitting apart, the back of my chair — our only chair — and my back against the table, that being the best hectoring pose I could find. At Mrs Forbes' entrance, Reuben the urbane European leapt to his feet and indicated a place on the bed. I guided her there. He made small talk in his gutturals. I waited.

They talked.

–You be about 20 what?– Mrs Forbes asked/told Reuben.
–28. Born 1908. The year King Leopold took the Congo– Reuben gave as full an answer as his priest/father had given him and smiled triumphantly.
–He was about that age when he came here too.– They knew whom they were talking about, so did I.
–Then how is your name spelt?– He spelt it for her.
–K-O-H-L– I wondered where all of this was going, for Mrs Forbes while she talked to Reuben kept watching me as the other woman would, meaning to say to you, "Don't worry love, I don't want him forever, just for tonight". I was not in the conversation and was not intended to be. This is the point at which the polite woman, intent on establishing suzerainty goes across and puts her loving hand on her man's shoulder, snuggles up, smiles at the other woman and forces her to a fumbling withdrawal, or where the not-so-polite woman, equally intent on correcting a slight, goes across with a knife, a fist, an open palm and chastises

the interloper for wandering without due permission into sacred ground, or where the more retiring kind, with similar intent as her sisters above, withdraws physically, slamming the door or not, forcing the loved one into action. I did none of these thing. I just waited, thinking to myself that Mrs Forbes is not so inept.

–That's a strange spelling. Where you get that spelling?– Reuben went into his European past.

–And you talk some other languages?– Reuben said "yes" and I waited for Mrs Forbes to ask him in her 'poor Forbes' voice, "Do speak in your foreign language for me". But she didn't ask that. Her next comment was:

–You really looking like him except for the colour. How come you have that colour?– I couldn't help smiling. The tick was turning into a toad. This was my victory, for Reuben was appreciating the transformation. This is the point at which the loving lover begs his love to extricate him. He was sending frantic signals to me. Let him feel what it is like to have the scales turned on you and the field interrogate you! I was the observer only. I would not be drawn into participation. He mentioned the Congo. Then Mrs Forbes let him off the hook and turned to me.

–You see dear, I have to know. He wasn't there. She couldn't look at him and say to me he is the one. You understand dear?– Of course I did not and I told her so.

–Go slower Mrs Forbes– I said to her. She backed up.

–Well you do know that they have chosen you?– Before I could deny it or counter this assertion in some way, she had gone on. –Everybody knows but I knew before and she knew that I knew. Picked it up as soon as I got back with the doctor, that you had taken over the lifeline. If you didn't have to run off, she might have completed the process there and then. I was so hoping that she would. I tried to keep away from you both, but then you had to leave and she told me to see that he was the right one. Poor me.– I now knew

72

Mrs Forbes' problem. Quite capable but scared of responsibility.

–So you now know Mrs Forbes?– I asked with more sarcasm than I intended because I could empathise with her, this unwilling beast of burden. I too wished that my cup could pass from me. She felt the rancour but she took no offence. She probably understood the source.

–Yes I know–, she answered. –The clue she gave was, "He's coming from far". He couldn't be coming from further, could he? The Congo.– Well. Well. I had gone to meet him. Couldn't the dying lady have been referring to the fact that I had gone to meet someone who had travelled a far way to get here and there really was no supernatural mumbo-jumbo here at all? New York was far enough and the old lady knew that I was going to meet a travelling guest. I let that thought dissolve: it had nowhere to go, nor would I bother to think about how I got the life-line, what had I done to get it, and I instead took in the two people sitting before me. Mrs Forbes had her crooked fingers resting on her bottom lip as if she was going to bite them. "Had she done it right?" she seemed to be saying. Of course she had done it right. That type is not inept, just lacking in self-confidence and wishing they'd never be tested.

Reuben was tired. Reeling out his life story in fifteen minutes to a little old lady with dubious qualifications who was checking his credentials for a purpose he could not see, left him too, questioning. A part he had written for himself was turning out to be his reality. It was time to ask himself, "What is this that I am into?" I was neither here nor there. I had had my greatest shocks before. I just sat watching his bowed head and her fingers on her lips. She spoke again, moving her fingers down to prop sorrow.

–She gave me this to give you. You can't stay here. I'll take you there.– Reuben perked up. I opened the note and read aloud: "Go to Marie. She'll teach you". Talk about cryptic!

No harm in pursuing it though. I always had an inquisitive mind.

–Where is this?– I asked Mrs Forbes.

–You know Congo Square?– she asked. Now how could I know Congo Square? I only knew how to find my way from my home to Mammy's and how to get to Franklin bus station. I couldn't even say that I knew Franklin. I hadn't left the bus station that day I went to collect Reuben. I couldn't say I knew New Orleans; my bus had dropped me at a bus station and I had waited there for my bus to Franklin, on my settling in visit.

–I know it very well– she said and lit into the biography of Mrs Forbes. Reuben beamed. His toad had turned into a princess. –Congo Square– he said, lifting up his head in stunned surprise. The connection missed her. It nearly missed me. I had somewhere, perhaps in my preparation for entering Louisiana's black culture, read of Congo Square but had never connected it with that other. Mrs Forbes went on about her days and nights watching Count X and King Y play there. That was where she met her husband, the Duke who still plays there from time to time. Reuben looked ready to kiss this lady of the royal family of jazz.

As if the communication had been to him, Reuben breathlessly replied after Mrs Forbes long poem:

–This ofcourse is it. We'll be ready when you are–

–Take the machine– she said to me as she left. This woman was not inept. Just so lazy that she refused to know. 'Poor Forbes' hanging in the back and forcing me up front as if I, not she, was the nurse! Really. 'Poor Forbes'? No sarcasm intended. Mrs Forbes got us a ride. Had Mrs Forbes, no longer the little tick, but dear Moses, arranged this before-hand? Whatever the sequence, before morning broke, I had left Eden, guided out by Mrs Forbes and Reuben's enthusiasm for her plan. It was months after, that I could fully appreciate the intervention of the venerable sisters.

I got over

Madam Marie was the brown version of Mrs Forbes — an ineptness which was not ineptness at all. Madam Marie gave the impression of being totally discomfited by the little problem of how to sleep us.

–There is space. You can sleep apart in two different rooms or am I to put you in the same room? You see dears, I don't know.– We glanced at each other and belled the cat.

–In two different rooms, Madam Marie.– Next day, the first item on our agenda was how to organise our lives so that we did not embarrass Madam whom we accepted, would be our hostess for some time. It was clear that we had to get married. Where would this wedding take place — in New York where my parents could preen? We decided that that was too risky. We couldn't yet release the recording machine — that was the message from Mammy through Mrs Forbes, and someone there might hear of our return and harass us. A small wedding it would be and my parents would be informed by telegram after the event. A small wedding takes no time to arrange. After three days of sleeping apart we were wed in Madam Marie's parlour and became the unit she found it easier to deal with.

What a simple solution to a large problem! And we had not even factored that in! Reuben could now apply for a permanent visa on the basis of his relationship with me and be free to seek employment outside of Columbia. In the weeks to come we were to understand that this was Madam Marie's way of operating — get them to solve the large problem by focusing on the small. Madam Marie was, like Mrs Forbes, short, fat and round. Apart from their colour there was one other apparent difference which we early sighted. Where Mrs Forbes tended to absorb slowly and let off slowly, Madam Marie's movements were fast. She took in speedily and let off speedily. One of the things Madam took in and let off was stories.

The port of New Orleans is a very active one. There are ships and sailors from every conceivable part of the world. Madam was acutely interested in those who looked most like us. The banana boats from the West Indies had a fair share of such sailors. These made up the bulk of Madam's clientele. She took from them their tales and quickly passed them on. There was laughter on the taking in and laughter on the giving out so that where Mrs Forbes tended to exude a dead pan stiffness, Madam had the air of twittering silliness. Her West Indian friends, Jamaican, I think, told her about Anancy, the spider. Where we here talk about Brer Rabbit, their talk was about Anancy.

Anancy had a magic pot. To this pot he would say; "Cook mek mi see". Madam told her tales in the speech and the accent of the teller. Anancy's wife couldn't understand why in this time of drought and hardship her husband was looking so well-fed. She determined to spy on him. Perhaps he was eating the little she could give him and eating at the table of another wife or wives. If this was so, she would drop him, for it was difficult enough to find food for the mouths of eleven children, why should she not add to their share, what a faithless husband and father now consumed? She watched him day and night, reorganising her chores to give her this time. Finally she saw. Anancy took a pot from under the dry leaves where he had apparently hidden it and said to the pot, "Cook mek mi see". The pot cooked him a meal. More days and nights of watching him convinced her that he really could make the pot prepare him a meal and that this pot was the agent of her husband's look of well-being. She would use the pot and food for the rest of the family, she told herself. Mrs Anancy as she had seen her husband do, ordered the pot "Cook mek mi see" and the family was given so much food that Mrs Anancy could store and not go to the field next day. But Mrs Anancy in her tidiness washed the pot. Next day, to Anancy's summons "Cook mek mi see" the pot made no reply...

She let that tale off on us. We laughed of course but felt, knowing Madam by now, that there was a message somewhere in it for us. What magic thing did we know? The recording machine ofcourse. Was she saying something about it? I certainly had not touched it for the two weeks I had been there. The first week was spent settling in and getting married. Now we were spending time in Congo Square and I was perfectly convinced that Reuben was right: he had found his family; he had found his tall oak with capillaries doubling back to home. We were now discussing forms of livelihood that could support his stay here. With his facility with European languages, the European interest in jazz and the desire of jazz musicians to be exposed to Europe, he could open a language school for musicians. We thought up various variants on this theme. Reuben was studying them.

By week 10 things had settled down and I was ready to make a space for my own work. Reuben's plans were bearing fruit and he now had his own interests to engage him. I went back, alone, to the sisters. I had been scouring and rinsing that tape before I left St Mary. I had done it well. Reuben had gone a considerable way with the faircopying and I took it over to produce the original of the first transcript here presented. Analysis it now was. And I went back to my scheme. File 1 — people — Lowly, Ezekiel, Silas, Donna Claire, the mistress, Ramrod Grant and ofcourse Sue Ann Grant-King. I do not know what made me go back to the recording machine and the reel that I had scoured and rinsed so well. Perhaps I had said

"Let me reconnect with this work by listening through again." Perhaps I had Ramrod on my mind. All I know is that I heard Mammy's voice on the reel saying something she hadn't said before.

They would hold me up on their knees: they had done so. They had sent me to Madam Marie and allowed me to continue my work. They had placed Reuben in his home and settled the visa problem. Let me take this leap in the dark knowing that I would not dash my foot against a stone nor be locked in that dreadful, aweful, confounding basement. This was what the story of the magic pot was about. Let me accept this recording machine as the magic pot. Let me suspend my own sense of right behaviour and not worry about keeping around me what is not mine. Let me just eat and leave the rest to them. I didn't bother Reuben about my find — he was busy enough tapping his roots. I said nothing to Madam and believed that I showed no sign of change in my behaviour to either one of them. I just prepared myself to transcribe once more and prepared myself for a new kind of devotion to this work. This instalment was shorter than the first. Within two weeks I had caught what I call the 'current all' for it does appear that magic pot cannot be cleaned.

The additional data reads:

My Grandpappy was a thinking man but he ain't know no word called 'slave'. He be thinking though and Massa Sutton he always be raising questions with him: "Moses" Massa Sutton he like to say. "Wish I was you. Nothing to worry you. You gets your clothes, you gets your food, you gets your house, you gets your children. Massa Sutton, he pay. Me, I gotta be wracking my brain; gotta be ever asking myself where to get cheaper money, where to get that better price; this here shipper, he be fair? It is a hard life Moses." Come the day Grandpappy say, "Only difference Massa

Sutton, you sleeps on the featherbed and I's on the moss".
You sleeps on the featherbed and I's on the moss.   With
that one saying the learning start.

Massa look at him strange and silent. From that day Moses
could do no right. Strange and silent be Massa that day.
Massa Sutton he be thinking. And Moses he don't give up
no thinking neither. Evening Moses gits home he tells them
others. Massa Sutton he say such and such and I say such
and such. And they be saying "Right word. Massa Sutton he
do be treat us reasonable like, quick with our rights be they
food or rations. Two suits of clothes and we be fairly warm
when the winter comes. Over yonder there be that pig-
stealing lot, we got no call to do that. He treat us right well
but in a manner of speaking and from pure logic, you be
right Moses. He do be sleep on the feather and we on the
moss." And the word like the gospel through the place, my
Grandmother say: Massa sleep on the featherbed and we on
the moss. And they be thinking and be thinking even while
they planting that sugar cane, chopping that sugar cane,
dropping that corn seed, breaking that corn — Massa sleep
on the featherbed and we's on the moss. A man be thinking,
it can show in his face; can mess with his work for his eyes
ain't seeing good and he ain't be singing and laughing, for
all that power he would use done gone to his brain pan to
help with the thinking. All them mens just be thinking and
Massa Sutton be thinking too. They can feel that thinking.
Massa look at them strange and under his eye and he be so
silent with Moses, but not a word yet called 'slave'. Things
done get to my Grandpappy, my Granny say. This silence
twixt him and the master when first it was Massa want his
head clear he open up that head to Moses, Moses he put
this word to the front, that to the back, this one twixt this
and that and set the master's words in the right and proper
fashion. Massa cast out that word, Moses take it, examine

it, be it no good, he throw it out; can it be fixed, he fix it and put it in a right spot and so. The thing get to my Grandpappy, Man, my Grandma say. He be getting frightened. Silence ain't good. Men have no words could talk with their fists and hell and damnation if the wrong fists connect. And if the wrong fists connect, whose fault it be but that of my Grandpappy on account of the word he throw back to Massa. So he leave. That's when the word 'slave' come to be spoke.

He just get up cool like and go. You know how when the prophets of God get the word — Go down to Nineveh and preach me that word (though that one really was the disobedient kind and needed a night in a whale's belly to get him to do right). Leastways, my Grandpappy move silent but it weren't silent Massa go for him. Go for him with those dogs that were his friends. With them poor white trash Massa Sutton did class as no count before Moses. My Grandpappy tired and lay down by the bayou, under one of them big spreading oaks when he see all of this anger before him and he do a very foolish in the face of those feelings. Moses run. And the chase begin. Man and horse, dog baring their teeth, running down one tired man who want nothing more than to stop the silence and the trouble it could bring. They catch him like a common thief and carry him back home. Oh Lord!

Shame set him to deeper thinking; why a man can't leave to avoid trouble? Shame must be set Massa to clearer talking for he tell my Grandpappy plain and straight: "You is a common slave. You is mine. You be bought and paid for. You have no right to go off as you please." Bought and paid for by somebody else! Dear Jesus, bought and paid for. Have no self! And that was when the great talking and the great listening begin. Then was when them old folks, my Granny say, begins to hear cannon shot; begins to hear bout slave and free; begins to hear bout Massa Lincoln; begins to hear my Grandmother say, within their inner ear bout people like them who can sit down and write down what they think. Ole Pappy must be hear bout that and it settle in his mind. He run off again. This time he know what he running to but he didn't get far. Massa Sutton and them hang him from one of them oaks. Old Grandpappy hanging like black moss, like a gypsy-style earring hanging from one tree lobe. That never happen before. Massa Sutton so shame, he do away with himself. Do away with himself. And that never happen before neither. He and Grandpappy move together from they small.

And here were some new people for me to put on my list — Grandpappy Moses, the thinking man and Massa Sutton, the suicide.

There was nothing else after this. I touched, I pushed, I stroked, I, focussed and projected myself but there was nothing. Nothing else on the recording machine for me to work on and transcription was what I felt like doing then. What would I do with myself? I loved housekeeping, particularly cooking but there is an easily reached limit on how many exciting meals you could make on what was left of my stipend and of the pocket money Reuben had taken with him from New York to St Mary. True Madam would take nothing from us for our quarters and we didn't force her to — we would when we could. Still, cash was really too tight for creative cooking. So I was bored. I stepped out a bit with Reuben next door to his Congo Square haunt and the jazz joints he was discovering. Up Rampart St, down Rampart St. Up Basin St, down Basin St. It was a world of men, horns and uprooted women, strange music for me and delightful music for Reuben.

Hanging out was not to my taste. I preferred the one to one relationship, so I spent more time sitting around in

Madam's parlour talking now and again with her guests or thumbing through old music scores. In this occupation I made the alarming discovery that there really is something called relaxation. I was relaxing and beginning to like it though I did wonder whether I wasn't being a little worthless. I had never had so much time on my hands! Couldn't I even get me an undemanding job like store clerking, something gainful, some sort of job out there in the street where Reuben spent so much time. Employed by whom? Well, couldn't I compose a poem or write an essay? I didn't wonder long and was pleased at that for it meant that I was really relaxing. I felt in step with my group and liked the feeling. That was how Madam and Reuben behaved: they didn't worry that there was little work and little money. For Madam, another boat would turn up; for Reuben, just being was learning and learning was living.

* * *

A specially interesting crew turned up at Madam's — West Indian people from Jamaica mostly. Seems they were regulars. They loved to sing, so did Madam. Folksongs they called it. Sometimes it was Irish, English, Scottish melodies. "Kathleen Mavoureen the grey dawn is breaking/the horn of the hunter is heard on the hill," one would rise with a far away smile on his face and the others would join him. Craving harmony, there'd be a call, "Tenor-man, tenor-man come in here" and one or even all would forsake the tune and move to the tenor. They had fun. They were not at all like their compatriots around whom I grew up. Madam would intercept with whatever their song brought to mind, "In the sky the brought stars glittered/On the bank the pale moon shun/And t'was from Aunt Dinah's quilting party/I was seeing Nellie home", in her squeaky little quick asthmatic voice. Much clapping would follow and "Teach me that Madam" if they really liked the song. Even me would then join in and learn and we would sing until we tired of it. And so it would go on, one side singing, then Madam singing and somewhere in this concert which came with these Jamaicans we would all be singing.

There were times when there was a great dispute. "But Madam that's our song" or "Fellows where'd you hear that. That's ours" and the battle royal went back and forth with Madam telling how far in her distant past she had heard it and it couldn't possibly be West Indian, "Who carried it to you?", and they would counter in a similar vein. One occasion for great dispute was the entry of "Just before the battle mother". I fell totally in love with that song. A little man — Ben — , he came to mean a lot to me later, the quiet retiring kind. Ben got up and started:

Just before the battle mother
I am thinking most of you
While upon the field we're watching
With the enemy in view
Comrades brave around me lying
Fill'd with thoughts of home and God
For well they know that on the morrow
Some will sleep beneath the sod.

They let him sing on.

Farewell mother you may never
Press me to your heart again.

Madam joined him in what became a duet, for the others left them alone. It was like he was singing to her real mother and that both he and that mother, Madam, knew that his number was up.

But oh, you'll not forget me mother
If I'm numbered with the slain.

The applause was tremendous. No clapping. Each of those men went into his past to tell us the circumstances under which he had learnt that song. "It was my father's song. He couldn't sing but mother was a fine contralto, singing at all the concerts around. When she sang that song, you knew that something great had just happened between them. She sang for him. mother died with the last of us. We dared not sing that song in the house."

"You know how parents can be stern when they are bringing you up. Licks every other day, 'for your own good.' Carry water, feed pig, look wood and go to school and if you are ever late, teacher beat you and you get home and your parents hear about this and they beat you again for disgracing the family by behaving so badly that teacher had to beat you, though your getting to school late and shaming them was their fault. Grandfather, Pappy Roll, he lived with us. He was the one person in my boy life that was not in the beating circle. Boy, just about any big person could beat you. Pappy Roll was too old to work. He just sat in a corner of the house smoking his rope tobacco, in his clean khaki clothes, singing that song. When he died that corner was my piece of peace. The song came out of it and comforted me in my times of greatest need."

And so on. One sweet sad poignant memory after another. Madam said that her folks told her that civil war soldiers passing by could be heard singing that song like they knew they were marching to their death. The crew didn't argue: they apparently had no past for that song as publicly sad and therefore as large as hers. But I didn't stop dealing with what had happened. I couldn't get the shared experience of those two sets of negroes from two different parts of the world out of my head. I couldn't get it out of my head that Lowly and Mammy had been buried to the strains of the same song —

Upon the hill, the rising sun.
It is the voice that calls me home.

Ben, the conjuror of these journeys into the past had said nothing. His memory was so deep and painful that he didn't talk though he more than anyone else, I sensed, wanted to be rid of that memory. Ben was going to be in my corner. I needed him. We would help each other. I would help him through that memory and he would help me find some memories, but I would have to move slowly. It couldn't be this time; but when he came back, and he would, provided he could stay alive with that memory, we would work together. Before I could think through a strategy for reaching Ben, I was pushed centre-stage.
Unwillingly. Again.

There was another community song game that Madam and her West Indian crew played without giving it a name. I called it in my mind, 'You can't catch me'. Madam might sing, "Swing low, sweet chariot". They might laugh at her, "We know that". She would start the opening bars in the orthodox time and they would sing along with her, then she was nowhere to be found, for she was carrying her notes over hill and dale, jumping in the sky and dashing into the sea, and they couldn't catch her. A signature she laid down. That's all they could hold. She had run away far, far, far, with the full name.

Madam's stronghold was the tune. They couldn't enter that without the proper key and they didn't have that key. Theirs was the lyrics. They loved to sing about John Crows. Madam and I didn't know what were John Crows, so although we could hear the lyrics and catch the tune, the song had no meaning for us. They could without notice change the words of the song — "John Crow seh him a parson pickney / Can't work, can't work pon Sunday". What was that supposed to mean? John Crow said anything

87

that any singer wanted him to say. It was confusing. And difficult for us to join in. It was after one of these sessions when Madam had totally non-plussed them — I think she was doing variations on 'Steal away' — I saw them go into a huddle like fellows on a football field and saw them open up with smiles on their faces: they were so sure they were going to win! Together they gave a low groan... Hmmm-mmmmmmmmmn. Then one sang or started to sing: "Sammy dead, Sammy dead, Sammy dead oh."

He/they didn't get far. I felt my head grow big, as if someone thought it was a balloon and was blowing air into it. My shoulders rocked like a little paper boat trying to balance itself in the sea. You need feet to help you balance. Mine had grown stiff and my body slid from my chair to the floor, fluttering like a decapitated fowl. And I spoke. I was seeing things as if on a rolling screen, a movie screen. I saw the yam vines, light green on the pale yellow bamboo sticks; I saw the big brick oven; I saw the tombs, the barbecue; I saw the sand-dashed house, the tangerine tree close by it, rabbits opening their noses and sniffing and gobbling grass inside their meshed house; I saw the rush-seated chairs; I saw the green basin with the red flowers at its side; I saw the goblet sitting in it. I saw my Granny in her many layered garb. I saw me. A baby no more than nine months, in her arms. I saw her putting that baby in its crib. I saw the baby rise, holding onto the crib rail. I saw my Granny reach for that baby. I saw her fall before her hands could connect. I saw her there on the floor. I saw her watch that baby for hours. I heard that baby whimpering in fright. I saw that baby sleeping the troubled sleep of the emotionally exhausted.

Madam motioned them to leave me alone. I saw myself on the floor. I saw the men around me. I saw Madam's encouraging smile. I heard myself talking to that company in a baby's voice, as if a nine month old baby can talk. I saw space. I stopped talking. My head had returned to its normal size. There was no stiffness any longer in my legs but I was so drained. I just sat there. Madam indicated to them that they should let things be, so I sat there unable to move without help and with no help forthcoming. Then it was prophesying. I went on with the weak no-go body into prophesying. I looked at the faces of the men sitting around me and I saw stories. I saw long deep stories, stretching back and back on stacked, ruled, six by eight cards. The first cards said 'name', 'place of birth', 'date of birth ' I read that off for nearly all of the men gathered in that room. Ben's card said 'place of birth = Louisiana, St Mary'... I let that pass.

The silence in that room was deep, almost deathly. I was too weak to read any more. "I am too weak now" I said to the gathering. "I have to stop. The others at another time." I stopped. The voice stopped but those cards remained in my head and I knew that I could peruse them at will when I was stronger. You can guess the rest. Madam and I didn't even talk over the event. She helped me to my room and went back to her guests. I don't know what she said to them. I couldn't easily hear what happened in the parlour from our rooms but if I had wanted to or had the power to, I could have strained my ears and heard. I was too weak for that. I needed sleep. I did hear her tell Reuben though — she had accompanied him to our door — "She has come through and taken away all my clients". She was joking but we all knew now, that this was it; there was no turning back for me.

I welcomed my husband with a flood of tears that had begun with the moaning and head banging of a dissociated child. He was still thinking of me as the resister, thought I needed to feel decent and was resisting my departure from my scholastic base. He was now trying to make a link for me between what was happening to me and the academy.

"There now, there now, no one has really given Jung a chance", he said. Poor Jung!. I had resolved the issue of my relationship to the academy way back when I decided to keep the recording machine and follow Mrs Forbes into New Orleans. You can hardly change more than that. Following Mrs Forbes to New Orleans, keeping a rare article which you know is not yours, putting the race on the line and leaving them to say they knew it all the time — "born thieves", "born shirkers!" It would have been difficult to explain the contents of the reel, but I could have found a story and remained in academia if I had wanted to. Jung! Parapsychology! Pah!

No. That wasn't where I was. Poor Reuben. The sobbing had a mind of its own and it would not stop long enough for me to tell him that I was a little nine month old girl watching the one sure link with love lying prostrate on the floor, unable to go for help, discovered after 24 hours of restless sleep; whimpering and hungry; patronised by whispering adults with versions of the theme: "De mother know sey him mother ha pressure, him ha no right go wey lef him wid de young baby"; shifted from hand to hand; passed over the coffin and watching the earth enclose my grandmother.

My grandmother lived on a hill far away from the road. Below us was Mass Bobby — he'd play with me sometime, chucking me under the chin, staring into my eyes and smiling sweet nothings at me, or sending me scampering off on my knees to retrieve a windmill that he had made for me. He was a regular visitor to grandmother's house. Her house was big. Comparatively. There were three bedrooms — one room for the girls, one room for the boys, grandmother's room, an entry, a dining room, a pantry and a verandah. My mother was the youngest and the last to leave home. All the children had travelled yet grandmother had not filled their rooms. They were their rooms and should be available to them whenever they came and for as long as they wished. They never came. I was her six children.

The village was not sympathetic. It was ridiculous, they thought, for an old sick woman to remove herself from the company of a boarder or a tenant especially when people needed rooms to rent. Grandmother had workers. She was a farmer, a miller of sugar and a baker. Grandmother felt that high blood pressure was just the occasional spinning of the head and never heeded pointed observation that she was not the only one who knew how to plant cane, mill it and use its sugar to make sweet meats. Mass Bobby could more than manage, they said. Grandmother never listened.

Fortunately for me, Mass Bobby continued to love us and check on us every morning. He had checked on us early Sunday morning and we were alright. If for him 'check' hadn't meant a long face to face conversation, I'd now be dead. On his arrival on Monday morning, the windows were as he had left them and as they should be at that time of the morning — open. I heard Mass Bobby call. Weak from fear, from loneliness, from hunger, from whimpering, I couldn't hold my eye lids open long enough to take in the entry of the whole form. I can only see that big leather shoe laced up past the ankle of the foot, coming through the window, and trying to find a place on the washstand to land without sending the basin and the goblet in it crashing to the floor.

I fainted in relief. Then began the hustle and the bustle; the covering of mirrors, the emptying and refilling of water barrels, the shavings curling up from the wood, the smell of varnish, the shape of the coffin, the satin arranged inside it, the rosettes of many colours, the digging of the grave, the raucous voices, the white rum which grandmother would have ordered out of her yard if she could, the song — 'Sammy dead, Sammy dead, Sammy dead oh'. I wanted to contradict, to respond to their call *"Ah who sey Sammy dead?*

Sammy no dead yah. Sammy gone a.." but I couldn't talk, moreover I didn't know where my vibrant grandmother was gone, for that thing lying as stiff as board certainly was not her. All I could do was stare.

I was quiet and they said I was a good baby. I was called good and quiet for about nine months by Miss Ros, Mass Bobby's wife. Grandmother had an account in the government savings bank to which Mass Bobby was a co-signator. He used this to bury her. She had left the addresses of her children with the post mistress but with her body discovered so late, she had to be buried within three days which didn't give them enough time to get from the four corners of the earth to their mother's funeral. They came late. Understandably. My mother wasn't one of them. Some problem with her address.

My aunts and my uncles came and left. They too declared me a good baby. That good quiet baby was now raining tears on her husband's knees. Only now it was safe to know the loneliness and the despair, and to react. She sent money to take care of me; she sent parcels; she came when I was 18 months old. She dismissed those days: she never talked about them. It was my tears that cleaned those gravestones of years of accumulated muck and showed me that story. It angered me, angered me deeply, that she had not left the door open for me to say thanks to those people who had cared for me in those crucial years.

Now that I was no longer weak and crying, I decided to go back to New York and confront her. Reuben and I talked about it. What was the use? Could I get any more truth about the situation from her than I already had. Confronting her meant that I wanted to destabilise her. I could only morally do that if I was willing to devote time to helping her reassemble herself. And what about him, Reuben wanted to know. All the talk had been about 'her'. Wasn't he as guilty? Could I, Reuben wanted to know, handle the collapse of two. Give thanks. I was cleaner and lighter than I'd ever been before, I knew that. My practice was about to establish itself. Why didn't I just give thanks and press on? Why not!

Louisiana

I seem to have given up working on the recording machine. It must be months now since I sat down to do any such thing. Transcribing is of course not all together in my hands but that should not mean inactivity for I could analyze and hone the existing transcript into a history essay. Fact is, I have become worthless. I am not writing. I am becoming worthless in other ways. None of them a worthlessness that I mind but I can still think like my mother and know that what I am about is worthlessness. Workless is worthless and you see I do nothing. Nothing at all. I don't even think. I walk about with my husband, now my source of financial support. I do not even ask him about the nature of his business. My mind is on vacation: the rest of me sits around in Madam's parlour singing and talking with her guests, still mainly West Indian and though that mind knows that I am now a celebrity with them and that they are waiting, it does nothing. I too wait. A different waiting from that in St. Mary. There I didn't know what was the expected end. Here I know precisely what is expected of me. New Orleans is different in that way. There is another difference too. Here I know that I can deliver. I don't know when or even what, but I know that I will deliver.

Things are happening with me myself too: I am changing. Mrs Forbes came to visit and in her clumsy way gave voice to this change. She informed me and the world that I had 'got over' — "She wouldn't do it for us. It took some West Indian men to get her over", she announced to the parlour, embarrassing Madam, I think, by the revelation that she had been discussing me with her. Mrs Forbes hadn't been there when it happened. She hadn't seen Reuben; she could hardly have been in contact with any of the crew, so she had to have been told this of my business by poor Madam. No problem. At least now I know from the horse's mouth what St. Mary had been expecting of me. I know too from that same horse, that there is a name for that state in which your body is depressed into physical collapse and something else is activated, rather like an injection needle is pushed forward and the shell in which it resides, recedes. 'Getting over.' I prefer to call it hegemony of the spirit. I had experienced hegemony of the spirit. I could again and would. This is common knowledge around here and my mind and I are being left to the 'fullness of time'. That's a phrase from Madam. She is biblical.

I had put the question of my inertia to Madam, more out of academic interest than out of any deep dissatisfaction with my state, or any desire to change same. Madam didn't exactly tell a story this time. She read me one. We were alone; she just got up and read. Took her Bible and read. It was the creation story. Genesis one. I didn't have to think long about her message either... "And God saw that it was good." This refrain occurs at the completion of nearly every stage of creation. Madam was pointing me to the action of being totally satisfied with step one before taking the other steps. Remarkable! My self was on a kind of sabbath, evaluating stage one and resting/strengthening and absorbing the lesson there before tackling stage two. Not to worry, she seemed to be saying. I wasn't worrying. What a rare find though, this notion of the sabbath. I have taken to reading the Bible. I know that I am, with this, further away from the self I knew than ever, but if it is so, then let it be so.

Other changes have been taking place. They are relatively small things. My hair for instance. I no longer press. I don't know if this represents spiritual or intellectual movement or just plain convenience but there it is: my hair is natural and untouched. And I wrap it. Reuben says I look like Nefertiti and I like that. Sometimes he looks at me with my head swathed in cloth and becomes so distracted that I think he is seeing someone closer home than that Egyptian lady but let that be too. And I no longer wear slacks. That too might be convenience. I now sew my own clothes — I still operate a tight budget. I can't cut a pair of slacks; I can stitch together two pieces of cloth, the length from my shoulder to my ankle, cut and stitch on a facing and fell the hem and the inside seams of the resulting garment. So my dress style has changed and I look different. I am also now very observable in the streets. I was never as tall as my mother nor had I before her bearing. With my headdress and my long dress, I know I present a dignity rather like hers and an aura which turns heads. 'Another Madam Marie' I hear them say, though I have done absolutely nothing, have none of Madam's credits to my name. I take it in my stride and wait. I know what they mean. Madam is stocky and brown; I am tall and as black as black can be. It is not a physical resemblance they see. They are the seers. I won't let them hasten me towards my future though.

The Bible is taking up my time: it fascinates me. I'm glad Madam brought it into my life. I take it up and let it open itself as it will. Madam says there's another way. There's more to that comment than meets the ear but I will have to sort that out later. 'In the fullness of time.' Right now there's a pay-off in doing it my way. For instance me and the Elijah/Elisha story: here is definite recorded proof that what has been happening to me has happened to someone else before. A mantle had been passed before. No para-psychological theorizing here. And the bonus: all Bible-reading people, and they are many, know this and therefore and therefore know that I am not strange. This I need to know. And that passage just ups and hit me right between the eyes. The Bible opened itself to that passage and it jumped right from the page and just hit me right between the eyes. It was meant for me. Earlier I had met the transfiguration — 'Let us build three tabernacles'. Two dead people talking to a live one, just like Mammy and Lowly and me. And then now this Elijah/Elisha story, mirroring another aspect of my phenomenon. These Bible passages, serendipitously found, are for me: the message lies deeper than I can now comprehend but I shall meditate on them and shall neither take up prophesying nor meet those ladies in the recording machine until I have their full meaning round about me.

August 1937

Summer is here. The good Lord knows why he taught me to make and wear the clothes I wear. God, it is hot. Completely different from New York. This is steam heat. Now I know what a flannel suit feels like when you cover it with a rag and slowly push a hot self-heater over it. The Redeemer be praised for this head gear: it keeps the perspiration from falling into my eyes and my loose garments allow the little air measured out to us here in New Orleans to pass over my body and keep it from being smothered by my sweat. This is not the foreigners' response. All of New Orleans is hot sweaty and perspiring and sitting on its stoop. Conversation, like skirts lifted to fan legs, bits of cardboard to fan necks and bosoms, goes from side to side, up and down, in and out. In this flurry I hear about the witch of Endor. These too are biblical people. Another miracle in my life. One day I know no one who reads the Bible; another, everyone I know reads the Bible. I have a vague recollection of having known and felt sorry for that lady. I check her out in Madam's concordance Bible and my emotions embark upon some intense work. I am so sorry for the lady and her kind. She had been given special powers — she could and did call up Samuel — but she was chastised for using them. Why give her these powers if she is not to use them? I ponder and cogitate over the whole thing. I felt. Dissonance. Self-pity too, although I had yet to use my own powers. And then I am forced to think — why really have I made no effort to use these powers. Why? And I had to admit. Fear. Fear of admonition — the fate of that witch. I glance at Madam Marie. No sign of fear or dissonance there. Come to think of it, there was no sign of these in Mammy either. They obviously know something I do not. Foolish thought. As they say here "They forgot more than I'll ever know".

Madam knows that my glances are lines thrown out to engage help but she is not biting. This is something I am to figure out for myself so I spend some more time pondering, some more time sitting on the stoop perspiring, being dried by my clothes, listening to conversation ebb and flow, whoosh, woo, whoosh woo, like the waves upon the sea and my mind goes back to Elisha. Certainly followed Elijah around like a leech after his call. Wouldn't let him die without passing that mantle. Man of God really wanted power. Now why is he a prophet and not a witch? And he even called wild beasts down on the teasing children! Why should that unfortunate lady be ashamed of herself and Elisha not? Then I saw it. 'Man of God', I had said. Elisha took his orders from God; the little lady was running a private enterprise, her own corner store, stoking her own fire. Prophets wait for God. Elisha must have been grey-bearded with waiting for Elijah to be promoted and he to be appointed in his place! Nobody turns on prophets nor do they turn on themselves. They wait for God's orders. That makes the difference and I saw Peter, poor 'winjie' human — mother's word — making an effort to be useful, practical and controlling — "Let us make three tabernacles", when the higher authority had already made those tabernacles and put people in them, so much so that the occupants had long since passed on or were about to pass on. I laughed and had to share with Madam. "That's why we are so fat", she said. "We eat while we wait." I was waiting for a higher command. That's it. I vowed then and there to be a vegetarian seer.

October 21st 1937

The weather is reasonable again. I am sewing these long black woolly garments to wear under the loose fitting gowns which have been my salvation in New Orleans' summer. My outfits with every evolution bring Reuben closer to something he wants to remember. There is that pucker of his brows, but that is not what I want to record. What I want to write down here is my determination to begin seriously recording again. I feel that things are going to happen which are going to take me away and away and away from the analysis of those ladies' testimony and from writing that history. I fear that I might only be able to put down the facts that come to me from them. They are facts. I defend that, though I can't prove them to be so. I must commit them to paper while there is still time. That is my determination. Meanwhile I wait and write what comes to head when I feel like it.

Ben's boat come in and Ben came. That was two days ago. Wednesday. It is my vegetable gumbo day. Reuben is not yet a vegetarian. I am slowly bringing him around to it. On Wednesdays, by prior agreement, he eats what I eat. These are my particularly pleasant days. I sail out to the farmers' market and inhale the array of colors, smells, life, of the vegetables. I find myself humming unafraid, *Sammy dead*, and getting whiffs of something which grew, perhaps grows profusely in my grandmother's yard in my Jamaica. The penny royale. I have learnt to cook Louisiana style. I dare you to ask for crab or fish after you've had my gumbo. You just don't miss the flesh. Any day now Reuben will be totally vegetarian. But I digress. Ben came back. He wanted to talk. "OK. Great", I said to myself in anticipation of our mutual therapy.

Ben's story is so accessible. All I needed was her name. And Ben, dear Ben, is so cooperative. "Her name was Lilieth" was his first sentence. And I continued. His cards written in clear cursive, heavy stroke down, light stroke up, the pen nib cleaned of any excess ink, that firm fist moving with easy motion, with my rhythm 'til the cards and my mind are one: Name = Benjamin Johnson. Place of birth = Louisiana, St Mary, Jamaica. Date of birth = April 20th 1901. Life story... "She was very bright. Under your hand she matured into a fine mind that had just passed her final examinations and so well that a place in college was assured and free. But you had taught her more than books and that too had matured and was blooming. That's when you were playing it, *Just before the battle mother*. That was when she came to tell you. You will never forget the position of the sun in the sky that day. High. You will never forget the angle of the shade of the apple tree. Hardly a shade. Very little shade on the small flight of stairs that took her up to your verandah through the doors thrown open today for air and into your grandfather's rocking chair from which she made her understated statement:

–Anybody here?–

–No– you said. You didn't stop playing. You had guessed. Young fruit carries a smell of its own.

–Speak freely–, you say, lumps in your throat, your feet pumping hard on the pedals of the organ, your hand holding the notes down a little longer than you should. You were single. You could have married. You liked her. You had no strong objections to having a child. You might even have wanted that child if you could hold her and feel your germinating seed, but you couldn't touch her. Not with

103

the living room door open, because you were the head teacher and she was your student. You couldn't find the energy to get up and close that door, so you continued to sit on the organ stool, to pump the squeaking pedal — eeek, eeek, eeek and to work your fingers on the keys, pushing your chest out and your shoulders up. You sang. Just as if she wasn't there. You sang — 'Just before the battle mother/I'll be thinking most of you... ' You didn't even know when she left."

Ben was studying me. Watching me steal his thunder. It must have been something for him. He came to me wanting to talk and who was talking? "What else do you know?" He spoke quietly, in wonder rather than in the annoyance to which I thought he had a perfect right. It was as if I was waiting for those words like diarrhoea for a chamber pot, the words rushed out of my mouth so!

–Teacher what ah going do, please Teacher– and with those words the moan of the frightened bird of a child.

–Lilieth I don't know what to say. What is to be done? How far are you on? It doesn't matter. What shall I do?– rhetorical questions under the sound of the organ. Then the sobbing under the notes of the organ for a life that had spelt foreign travel, further study and maybe somewhere down the line a settled family with this said Lilieth or someone like Lilieth, for you liked her, really did, sobbing over the notes of the organ.

–Lilieth, I'm thinking– Ben, you said ten years too late for you were thinking and would have reached the point where even without her touch you could see your way to speeding up your life.

–I can't wait.– I said for Lilieth who ten years before had laid her case and retired for judgement.

–Everything is packed for college.– "She couldn't wait for your growth Ben", I said, then I physically got up and lay on the nearby couch with my legs apart. There is so much pain. I scream. So hard Madam rushes in and covers my mouth much as had been done to Lilieth. Ben slides to the floor and like I did a half an hour or so before, rushes into nonstop speech.

–Give me time. Give me time. Give me time. I will not be forced–, he shouts, then much more softly:

"I would not be forced into action, so they took her down to Port Maria. That was the end of her. I wasn't afraid of them. I went to the funeral. Report whom? There was talk of reporting me. What evidence had they. And report whom? Me or the doctor. Mother Stuart had enough respect for her granddaughter's reputation to squash all of this and give Lilieth's death a respectable cause. She hated me. I wasn't worried. That is natural. Her family and mine had produced stars, hers rising, mine constant in the sky. Why should hers fall just because it was created female? I grieved with her intellectually, but I hadn't made the world, so the injustice meted out to Mother Stuart and her response to it did not bother me unduly. What bothered me the most was the nightly fornication with that dead child. And so it has been out of the school room as in."

Madam had not left me after my scream. As Ben drew to an end, we looked at each other and retired from his presence by mutual unspoken consent. I had done my duty I was saying, and she nodded mentally. My job was to help him re-live his painful past. He had to take it from there.

* * *

"How silently, how silently that wondrous gift to us is given" sings the Christmas carol. Silently and slowly. It is while I am writing the conclusion of my experience with Ben and feeling the silver in my brain that I am realizing that the call came. They talk about the clarion call, let me talk about the clarity call. Clarity is silver. A silver spear that

105

goes slowly from one side of the head and through to the other, leaving silver dust in its path. These particles of dust are absorbed into the brain and your whole mind becomes suffused with understanding. Slowly and silently. An understanding that sparkles by degrees. As I am writing, I am remembering the faint jab of the silver spear entering my head at that soft point above my right temple. "My job is to help him re-live his past. He has to take it from there", it helped me to see. With this thought as a conclusion to that happening, I was then as sure as it is possible to be sure of anything, I know now, that my practice had defined itself and with divine blessing. The silver sparkles are about my head at their most powerful as I write and I know that I am not Elisha; I am not the unfortunate lady of Endor. I am a soothsayer, yes, but one who looks behind, sees and will see the past. I see that clearly.

And I am now seeing in sharper relief what the venerable sisters wanted of me. Still though, why after death? Mammy had been to death's door and back so often, couldn't she just have stayed and had her story written in the normal fashion? I'd still be doing it and at no cost to any of us, for the President had kindly offered to pay. She wants to hug her secret, let her. But let her and all and sundry know that the definition of my practice not withstanding, whatever behind-telling is to be done for whomsoever will have to wait until the Higher One has given me the orders concerning whose past to see and when, so you who are now tugging at my sleeve could just as well desist.

Monday January 27th 1938

Are female prophets allowed to have children? I must get my own Bible. I had to go across to Madam's concordance to ask Judith. Husband like me but no mention of children. I have been married today fully a year and no thing in sight. If it is to be so, then let it be so. Things aren't exactly flushy

106

but we are managing. We are even thinking of finding a house of our own. Perhaps then the child will come. Meanwhile I wait for all things. And I sew. I have found a cheap bale of black. Wish I were sewing for maternity. My smock pattern would only need a little more looseness. I now have several long black robes. I think I will wear black throughout the winter months.

February 1938

I felt them pulling at my sleeve all through this month but I was determined to stave them off. Mardi gras is an absolute necessity for Reuben. He is going to 'back enjoy himself' having through ignorance not played last year. The man has found his metier. "Zulus, Zulus, you said!" From the moment he heard of the Zulus he was in. So Reuben is going to be an African and in Africa and I am making his costume. 'All 'o body' — shades of my mother — will have to understand. Afterall they gave me this man.

March 1938

It was great. I never left the stoep but it was great. Perhaps I'll be on the road next year. No. That's Reuben's domain. I'll get more involved with the planning and the backstage work. Here they come:
Ah who sey Sammy dead.
I am coming. I am all yours but I won't go to the recording machine until I have prepared myself. I need to review the transcript and, if only in my head, understand the connections between the original and the last bit. This last bit was all about Mammy. Or Mammy's forebears. Now what do we know about that lady?

Next day

Much searching but I have found the people file. It is file 1. And I have found the sheets marked Sue Ann Grant-

107

King. Yes. She:

1) left Louisiana for Chicago. Worked there as a maid or some kind of domestic in a guest house.

2) married legally or otherwise Silas the boarder. Etc.

The pre-Chicago data is what I need. This I will retrieve and rinse and look at Mammy longitudinally, so two headings are really necessary at this stage of our information gathering and analysis, to wit:

1)Chicago 2) Pre-Chicago. Others will perhaps come later. Now, the 'pre-Chicago days of Sue Ann Grant-King' will involve me in looking at

a) the longshoreman's strike

b) the desire, inherited, it seems from Ramrod, to stay in Louisiana

c) being happy in Louisiana. She must have been since she said she'd rather be there.

Late March 1938

Did the new data help to flesh out these themes? They did not. This last tranche was all about Moses, Grandpappy Moses. I decided to work with what I had, and the data and I struggled like Jacob and the angel, through the washing of the dishes, through the trips to the market and even through a little bit of sewing. If Grandpappy Moses had heard about 'Massa Lincoln' in conjunction with news of a negro intelligentsia, then he must have met his end before or about 1863. Hurrah, another date. News came to Mammy through her Grandmother, Grandpappy's mate, so there must be a tradition of handing down family histories here. I might just hear more about the family then and about Mammy herself. I do hope she does talk about herself and her times because I would love to send some information of this kind back to Columbia in expiation of my crime. I am unhappy about keeping this machine. Perhaps I could extract from the manuscript the relevant pieces, make a collage of the data and send this to them with another state's or country's stamp. This shouldn't be so difficult. Reuben or one of his pals could easily do this. They are always off to Chicago. Mammy is the key. Would she be so kind as to give me a narrative plain and straight of her life and doings in South West Louisiana that I could send in this way to them? Some hope. I don't let them rush me; I won't rush them.

Ramrod intrigues me. He seemed so pivotal in the first delivery. Now nothing more about the guy. I have to take it that he is from the male side, for the portion most recently given to me relates just to the distaff side. Who can control Mammy? Only God.

I didn't get a chance to complete my meditation on Ramrod. Like a seed ready to pop jumps at your slightest touch on that pod and causes its lids to keel over, Mammy jumped into my ear on that misty morning when I settled in to listen. Thank heavens it was pancakes for breakfast. Anything heavier would have jumped too right out of my belly and on to the unfortunate machine. My goodness! The shells of my ears felt as if they had indeed keeled over with the pressure of my fingers on the play button. And so loud was the lady, I had to tone her down just to hear her words. The discordance induced by the volume was made worse by the mood in which she was speaking. Mammy was vexed. Was bitter. Vexed for two or more. She was that bitter.

–We never did go to the Catholic but they like everyone else used to find our home. Suppose they tell themselves they were helping out. To me it seemed like plain gawking. Where they going to find one family with so many sent to Calvary and it sitting down still, toiling and spinning more radiant than any of Solomon's lilies, a top spinning so quiet they can hardly see it move? They just want to see what kind of metal make us. Then there were those who want to

109

get us to go any place. Re-locate, free gratis and for nothing. Anywhere, just so they wouldn't see us. That place so shame of itself. And it ought to be. A woman! They do that to a woman!

—My mother got that thinking fervour from her father though she barely know the man, that's what they tell me. "Nice well settled man come courting when she sixteen", Grandma say. "Man not too settled nor so old she couldn't get to make a mark. And he could strike some good chords on that accordion, he come courting with, sitting right there on his back like a set of peacock feathers. Me? I'd have jumped at him. Pretty zydeco moves that man could execute. No ordinary sugar cane cutting man he. Cajun in the salt mines. Nothing strange and out of order about his singleness: the man's wife died and he ready to find another good woman and he choose your mother. Tell me now, ain't that storybook enough? Man could have danced and played til his fingers and toes drop off one by one. Your Ma would not be seen by him. Thinking woman! Them boats done set her mind to thinking. What that country like, what this country like and so on and so forth. Head full of thinking", is what my Grandmamma tell me about my Ma. "She be thinking that poor dear Ned Harris, he too yellow, hair too crinkly, nose too straight, he too everything. 'Man ain't from nowhere far', that's what that gal should say if she was honest. Ned just from round the corner up by Lafayette country. No boat to take."

—"Tongue-twisting and voice singing up and down, this man have stories to give her. Stories." 'Brer Rabbit', my Grandmother call him. Say she rue the day she let that gal find her way to New Orleans. "Man been to the high seas", my Grandma say she say he say. Been to Russia; been to South America. "He take her behind my back." I think that is the greatest wrong my Daddy do my Grandma. "Ring can keep my child? Or photo album? Pooh", my Granny cheops. "Full of himself. 'to look at while I on my ship'." I knew that photo album well. All left of him. My Granny was hard. My Mama was there too. My favourite photo is of him sitting on a chair, cutting his ten, she with her hand upon his shoulder. That is her wedding day. I could travel years back and forth with that. That man was my Daddy and nothing Big Mama could say could get me to stop loving him. But this is not my story. It is my Grandma's story and I could see it her way for all he really leave my mother was that photo book, talk of far away places, me in her belly and that song.

−"Must be the ship sink", Granny say. "Must be it drop clear off the map; must be he sail too far north or too far south, too far east or too far west." All my mother would do, was rub her belly where my head protrude and sing that song that so sad. My grandmother would sit for hours thinking about her little girl and singing that song she used to sing.

Green turtle sitting by a hole in the wall
hole in the wall
green turtle sitting by a hole in the wall
looking at the deep blue sea.

−And Granny would sigh, "Girl like a god-forsaken green turtle." Who wouldn't be. My Daddy one very alive man, kept alive, pickled in anger by my Granny. But it is her story. "Slow moving like she have no body at all, your mother would move. That singing voice connected to nothing. It worried me", my Grandma say, "this child would think she was nothing but water or air and let that stream — and we wasn't short of them — pull her to its innards. But you came", my Grandma say of me. "She hardly drop you before she be out of that turtle self and flying like a bird. Back into sugar cane. Girl work like it was the last days, like St Peter say 'who chop most, get first place on that ladder cross the sky and up to heaven'. Like a man, that woman work", my Grandmother say. "Would take no other man til men begin to think she be a man and pay mind to your Mama's thinking. Heh!" Granny say. "She think things can change. 'Hush chile'", my Grandmamma say she say to my Mama. "'Hush chile. He come back if he come back. You can't put the world upside down and hope somehow to shake him out. No sense in that.' Girl just look at me silent and be thinking: wages too small. Need not be so small. 'Just a few of us to feed. It look like we dying?' I say to her", my Granny say. "No answer. Girl make no answer", my Granny say. "'It shouldn't be that our little piece of land be snuck away for them old rotten sausage they be forcing us continually to buy.' 'Hush I tell her.' I clutch my heart. Ain't I been through this already? Ramrod he ain't moving either. Old ark's a movering but they sitting steady. That man just a ghost under that cotten tree there. Man in never ending competition with my Moses. 'Ain't moving. Gotta swing me right here.' Swing him indeed and leave me a widow two times, though I never shoulda say that for the one run and the other stay. Same thing with Mister Charlie. Run or stay, same difference, long as you answer back. Now this child... This child carry the same nonsense right into my house. Our house now one meeting house. Girl make believe my house now is a flaming flesh house, all them mens stealing in and stealing out. Discussing, discussing, discussing. Them men and them words push me into the wall in my house and me just hanging on to that wall like Massa Findlay mother portrait, holding my heart that leaping right into my throat, only I have no pearls to clutch to steady me. Girl even had me step off of that wall swinging my arms and believing them things she saying, that change can come."

112

–Read about the caneworkers strike on the Teche, my child? That's my Mamma's strike. Til now nobody seen the body, they tell me. Nobody know if that be the woman lynched down in Louisiana that have this state with Mississippi flying off to Chicago city. "Certain people", my Grandma say, "too sure that 'strange woman' throw she own self in the river. 'Ain't she been acting strange ever since she been back here Vinnette'", — Grandma name Vinnette — "big Massa, Massa Findlay, Massa Findlay wife say, the works overseer say." My Grandmother say she say "Hmmmmmmm" and hold her belly tight. And that is how I, the little orphan baby, come to be in a Chicago kitchen instead of fighting my fight upon the spot.–

Two days of listening and writing, punctuating, paragraphing. Not what I am looking for to complete my crossword puzzle but who am I? I merely listen and transcribe. After this, a blank. Nothing more. I can't say I am as distressed as I was last time. Disappointed yes, for I had expected something more fulsome on Ramrod instead of just this whiff. But we must be thankful for small mercies, mustn't we. I had so hoped, that hope which springs eternal in the human breast, to have Mammy talk about the things with which she was involved, instead I hear about her mother, Moses' daughter. One fighting lot though eh!

I cannot say that I deeply regret the end of this session for there is no lack of things to do. I love housekeeping and in that sphere, every day brings something new — a new pattern to try, a new recipe to try and Reuben is developing a circle of friends so there are new people to meet; people to eat your stew and say it is the best they have ever had. Then there are the West Indian men: they are a delight. We have not seen Ben. We certainly hope he has not, Judas-style gone out and hanged himself. We have had enough of this. All are sinners and have fallen short of the glory of

God. I'll tell him that if I ever see him again. I trust that somebody else has told him that by now. Or better, that he has learnt that on his own. No Ben, but lots of others, their file cards stacked in age segments with data thereon written in such clear handwriting, it has to be scripted by a teacher of penmanship.

Summer 1939

It is fairly quiet here. There have been hurricane warnings and shippers naturally are hesitant to commit their cargo to the elements. Apart from which, there is the war and not even so much the war as the sighting of the submarines in Caribbean waters, the waters of the green turtle. Madam calls those machines 'Jonah's whales', talks about the days of the revelations, of evil boxes opened up and their contents left to fly willy nilly all over the world. "The end times." Madam is very religious. She is also very sad. Money is short but that is not what Madam's sadness is about for she more than I know that in our line of business, business can never be bad for long.

I am not much of a talker, much less so Reuben, though he does try. He tells Madam about the advance these submarines represent; how Wells had dreamt of them and look what has come to be! Madam is unimpressed. What has come to be? Reuben is way out of his depth. All heart but quite incapable of finding the words to go along with the heart. If I were to worry, I'd worry about him. He could be put in quarantine. "Who? Me? German! I'm a jew. Don't you know my name? I am a refugee. I came here to escape the fury of the Fuehrer." He can't resist that non-joke/yoke. He'll manage. Not so Madam, the 'last rose of summer', left blooming alone/all her lovely companions ... Poor lady. Madam misses the songs, the arguing. But the war will end.

I miss my men but with the space their absence has left

in my head, it has room for other things. My Wednesday vegetable day is stretching. That day is now like years. From the moment I met her, I knew that the clear clean cursive on those note cards is hers. Perhaps because she passed before Mammy she has had time to learn composure or something like that and is therefore less rushed in her delivery. I guess there is human time and other world time — 'a thousand ages in thy sight is like an evening gone' indeed. Mammy is still working on human time, must be. She seems to fear that some obstacle could and will emerge from somewhere to derail her message, so pour it out, pour it out as fast as you can. No such thing with Lowly. Tomorrow will always be. Funny thing is, that in the first life she was the excitable one.

On which of my vegetable days did I first meet her? Can't remember. I must really start recording these events seriously. Here goes.

July 1943

'Ah who sey Sammy dead' had been playing in my head — by now our signature tune — and a loud clear accented voice said with measured pace, "Thank you for helping Ben." That was all. She was gone. Just that. I had no sense of loss or regret; I felt instead a connection that was here to stay and knew that whatever I was to get from her of her or of anything else, would come 'in the fulness of time' and that there was no point in either of us trying to force the pace.

She chose vegetable days to talk to me or vegetable days were chosen for us. She normally selects a theme — very nearly always one of my themes — and indicates that we will work on it on Friday. For these past how many years — three or so — she has been actively with me on Fridays, clearing up details — Dinkie mini, nine night, Portland, coon can. She laughs, "Coon, can. Can you see it?"

Patiently. "The coon can" and laughs again. We do the transcripts over and over again and my eyes widen. What a difference punctuation makes! With the punctuation marks in the places to which she guides me, I am getting behind the words. "Chimboraza, Cotapaxi took me by the hand." She says the words over, rolling them on her tongue, and I empathise with Mammy's picture of her, "They fall off your tongue so easy like fresh water down a clean man's back." Lowly loves words. "My mother died my father too/they passed like fleeting dreams." She gets me to say it too. I know it is my portrait. "I stood where Pococatapetl in the sunlight gleams." 'Why worry', I know it/we are saying, 'you will be taken care of.' Give thanks. If these transcripts make sense to any third person, bless her. It is her work.

Talking to Lowly didn't do very much for the gaps in my information but I felt her country, my country, Mammy's country, our country. I felt her anguish in the Chicago cloud; I knew the joy of being separated from the dead weight of the body; I went way past fainting. I grew to hunger for the jab of the silver spear. Feeling is knowing. That is enough. Life is good.

Late summer 1943.

The men are coming back. More men than before. Not just sailors now, employees of the United Fruit Company as well as farmworkers. These latter come in large numbers and make such a difference. Seems Madam has been able to pull the war around to make sense, for these new West Indian men, we hear, are being invited to come here to help with the war effort. We neither know nor care what that effort is, Madam and I. We see no war here; the men are involved in no such nefarious activity as far as we can see and we can see far. They come, paid for we think, by our government. They plough as is right. They weed the plants; they cut cane; they pick apples. We see them in their

116

coming in and in their going out. I see them on Saturdays through Tuesdays — not necessarily the same faces. I go to my vegetables on Wednesday, selecting with Lowly along the way what we shall do on Fridays. She has taught me well. I have the language pat, idioms in place. 'Ah chi chi bud oh/some ah dem a holler some a bawl.' Chi chi bud? What is that? Ask me another man, I'm well past that. Wednesday to Friday, we talk. She helps me phrase the questions I ask myself; Saturday to Tuesdays I am with my men cross referencing and verifying. With Lowly and the men, File 1 has some new names and along with File 4 which deals specifically with me, it is becoming relatively fat. I am knowing more about my men and where they are from and in the process, I am becoming. Language is the key.

December 15th 1943

Somebody has thrown water at Madam's roots. She is green again and Lowly is more like Mammy than I had realised. Sweeps you completely off your feet. With no introduction at all, no warning, Louise tells her story. In her clear low voice, slightly accented, just enough for you to guess another country, Lowly talks about Lowly. Why now when the men are so demanding, when their cards are being flicked from the top of my head to the nape of my neck like a card shark at work; when Madam is in power again and the laughter and singing have returned? Thank God for that. Sometimes I ask Madam why did men come to us before and what did we do for them. Today they come so mangled. Madam says it's the thing in the sea, which of course comes with the war and in a sense she is right. There is a distance, a separation that it brings; the separation of man from the charting of his future. It is as if once you stood on your edge, put your hand to your brow, spied over yonder and said, "that's where I am going" and you took your boat and set out for sea. Today the thing in the sea raises a stone wall. Scylla and Charibdis. But the men have to move. Coast people make their living from the sea. More still, the thing in the sea stops traders from taking food to their islands. Now they come, not excited at having travelled by their wont, but tired and wrought from crossing a great divide in search of that food. Another middle passage as unfathomable as the first, a middle passage that you consent to taking. What Lionel Campbell told us was nothing short of that. Hundreds of men squeezed on to a ship, a kitchen too small to feed more than the fifty for which it had been built; men stepping on each other's heads to get within reach of a ham sandwich; sleeping in the cold hallways in order to make it to tomorrow's supper, a young teacher opting for the sea for whatever reason and finding it too rough for him, jumps into it. I think of Ben. Thank you Lord, my Ben couldn't now be described as 'young'. Hunger, sleeplessness and the physical distress they bring; loss of dignity and the fear of the thing under the sea, come with the men. Lionel had prayed, "Dear God, I will even be a fish if that will bring food to my family". He had prayed wildly. A wild answer returned. An offer to a farmer to sail the questionable waters to an unspecified job. "Lord", he said "I asked to be a fish. You took me literally and are putting me in the sea. Let it be worth the while." Frozen fish came to us asking to be made into men. Is there a balm in Gilead? We give them their past and they take it from there. "There is a balm in Gilead", we said, putting our arms about each other's waist and stroking each other's back. There is singing and arguing again and this is when Louise chooses to tell her story.

I cleared some space between my many many tasks to listen. By now we knew each other well so punctuating was a fairly easy procedure. She said:

–I felt like the onliest little bird. You don't know the beeny bud, do you? A little bird. I felt like that. Perched upon the highest point of a burnt, blackened, leafless mango tree, staring into the dry blue sky, with absolutely no movement around me. It was no use writing to him. I doubted he could read and even if he could, and even if he couldn't and I didn't mind having someone read my letter to him, and even if I did know what to say, whom and how would I ask for paper on which to write to him, for pen and ink with which to write to him; whom would I ask for stamp or for the money to get stamps and who would post the letter for me or show me where to post it. Two weeks had gone and I was very sorry I had been so passive. I couldn't fight her I was so lacking! I shrunk at the noise and the embarrassment. That woman kept up so much noise! Throwing her skirt over her head and gesticulating. The men were laughing. He just stood in silence and so did I. Then he walked off to a corner, leaned like a broom would, against the unfinished wall, the upper half of his body framed by the green high mountain above which was the blue-blue January sky. I was standing alone, a sea of air around me, he quiet in one corner, she at the other, maddening herself, and the men in front of me bursting their sides with laughter. I was to act. It was my turn. I was to talk above the laughter of the men, the antics of the woman, with no lines and no rehearsal. Perhaps I was to move sideways to his corner and to him. The thought had barely crossed my mind before Father came and pulled the curtain down. Father in his black gown, face pink, foreign and sweating. "Colthurst, you again." Father was building two churches, one here in Above Rocks and one further down in St Mary, and Bailey — that was his home name — was with him on both sites. That "you again" petrified me. I looked at him. He was smiling in response to Father's comment. Could I then have looked closer, I would have seen not a grin but a grimace, not the pleasure of a pat on

119

the back, seen not the grin of the guilty but merely a meaningless gesture, the easiest response to the presence of Father in the internal affairs of the natives. Instead, I was overtaken by embarrassment at my inclusion in this male exchange as a third party. "Colthurst, I am going to take one away from you", Father continued. I saw grinning. Let me not be too hard on myself: I didn't have the experience to see a mask to put between himself and this foreign celibate Father and I froze where I was. I might be there today, Lot's wife, if the impelling variable had not intervened. Father's "Come with me Louise" forced me into motion. I went with Father. They told me that I had far too much sense, too much of a future to be a party to a quarrel over rights to a man who hadn't even asked for my hand. "Who was he to ask?" I did ask myself, but more on that later. Father took me to Sister Mary at Alpha Cottage in the city that very afternoon. I did not even get another peep at him. I did well at Alpha. My head was always quick. Sister ran a kind of placement service. She had contacts in America and knew where Catholic ladies needed household helpers. I think they would write and ask for workers. Whatever the contact, I was one of the first to go. I was good and justifiably selected for the honour. It helped that I had nobody to resist my going. Father said it was a good thing. I could better myself there and it really was. But cold! The place was cold! You've heard Sue Ann. No amount of warning could get me out of Silas' room. I went there for the warmth. In there was sunshine, was home. In there was Bailey, a Bailey I could more easily manage. Nothing happened that shouldn't. Sue Ann has already told you that. Now you'd better leave this and see to your husband and your clients.–

Another shipment of frozen fish, men, had indeed come in. This was Louise. She had matured with death. Pace and rhythm easy. Considerate. Hardly the breathless memory intruding into Mammy's testimony.

I am about to say that I could ask questions of her and not of Mammy, but I must re-phrase. I find it easier to ask questions of her. I asked her a question I had been saving for someone for years. The life-line. How does one, how did I get involved with passing the life-line from Mammy to me? She shook her head. "We really played with you. Awful. You put both your palms and both your hands on Sue Ann's, like Elisha with the Shulamite woman, rem-ember. You did that all on your own. We knew then for sure that it was you. That was the passing." Nothing more to be said. I remembered doing that. I was just frightened and wanted her to live. I wanted to give her some of my strength. I just did it naturally. Nuff said. She smiled and I knew that enough had been said.

I suppose my need is the great variable distinguishing Mammy from Lowly. She knew I would have difficulty with her references given her foreignness, so she was ready to translate and to entertain requests for explanations and even to give them before they were asked for. We thus, I suppose, established a question and answer pattern between us. I asked her niggling little things. I didn't know the 'beeny bud'. I asked her for a more detailed description sometime after I re-read her story. It came. The men had sung about it so I was doubly curious. 'Beeny', small. She gave synonyms: 'beeny', 'teeny', 'tiny' = small. She went on to further exposition like the Oxford dictionary. A nice 'small'. Not 'winjie' — I knew that one from my mother — which is skinny, a not so nice 'small', pausing for signs of miscommunication and setting this to right. What she knew, she knew well and imparted well and willingly. She behaved like this with the telling of her life story, so that I had a clear picture of the setting. She had been brought up in Louisiana, St Mary and she knew it intimately. Strange, for she had had to leave it at an early age. She had left it temporarily for holidays with her grandmother but the blight, 'vomiting sickness', she called it, wiped the whole family out in her absence and she had had to remain permanently in Above Rocks with her grandmother. Grandmother herself, soon after departed this temporal sphere. Hankering after brings a more intense knowledge of things? Feeling intensifies knowledge? Clarifies? If it was not possible to keep earthly touch with her kin and the spot where they had grown her, she could lock them in her heart and feed on them. Well masticated, digested material was what Lowly gave me. This intense child nibbling intensely on memories, the orphan so beloved by romantic tales caught the eye of Father who took her into his house. Holy Mary mother of God, her mother, Ann, the nuns, and the several sanctified men and women of the Catholic church held hands with the Grants in this child's head. She knew them well. Father, white, male, foreign, as ephemeral, as foggy as the smoke which made the cloud on which the Grant tribe with the Holy Catholic family sat, was her connection with the real world. Bailey/Colthurst threatened unsuccessfully to force this cloud into rain. Alpha was another cloud; Chicago another. But for Mammy and Silas the rain would never have shone in this child's eye.

Early 1944

Ben came back. Through the mail. He has gone back to teaching. His letters are all flora. He is in love. With a place. Somebody must have told him love is easier the second time around. I doubt whether we will ever see him here again in the flesh for Ben seems to have shunned the sea. Hiking is a pastime of his and when he is not reading books and sharing the information from them, he is walking in and out and up and down throughout Jamaica. I don't mind one bit. I get to know all parts of this my island and I can make geographic jottings on the cards of those of my clients who are from this part of the West Indies. I know the bun batty-bush — a pretty fern; I know the trumpet tree and how her leaves turn over to indicate the coming of the hurricane and ofcourse I can jump into any song: 'Solomon Granpa gone a Equador/left him wife and pickney out of door/Nobody business but him own'.

Madam and them continue to fight. They stole it, she says and insists on singing to their "Nobody business but him own", "Ain't nobody business but my own". I don't know if she or them know how well they sound together. A clash of sounds which is not really a clash — just an almost clash. I describe this for Reuben. "Jazz", he says "the sound of the cymbals" and he says the word "jazz" in a way that makes me hear and see two hands, two circles and a sound as they strike each other. I smile. "Soon you'll hear the trap drums" and he tries jazz with all of him, voice hitting voice, hand hitting hand, heel hitting shin, all in its own time, held together by one chord. Well there it is. Do they know they are making jazz? I think I am going to like jazz. More immediate for me though, is that when the boats to the West Indies sound off, they take me with them and I am sitting right here in New Orleans, Louisiana, yet searching grave-stones, stringing duppy bead, going into caves, eating mangoes and jackfruit there. I nearly re-named myself "Jamaica Ginger". This bottled drink and I are home for the travellers from the islands. I do feel like a warm homely liquid.

I understand from Louise and from Ben that I am from a place not too far from their Louisiana, that the New Bethel on my birth certificate is the same place as the Windsor Castle on my parents' marriage certificate and that my place is near to their Louisiana. My place in fact shares their Louisiana post office. I don't seem to have any blood relations there. I have asked Ben whether in his wanderings he wouldn't stop by there and check on Mass Bobby. I assume that Ben's sad past is tied up with this place that is so close to my New Bethel and from which his files says he originates. It would be painful for him to return to this area. I know that and I am not rushing him. Not by any means. Still I wish he would hurry. Am I being selfish? Yes, but it is true that nothing but an exorcism can come for him from re-visiting the scene of his love and the sin that accompanied it.

April 1944

My husband had ordered a pendant for our fifth wedding anniversary. We really needed to mark our change. It was delayed. Here it is on my birthday. Things have been happening to me and ofcourse to us ever since Mammy's death five years ago. That fellow, Metamorphosis has been constantly with me. With the arrival of Louise his activity peaked. My pendant celebrates that peaking. Stand if you will. Let your arms hang loose in front of you. Now put the tips of your index fingers and the tips of your thumbs together. Your extremities now form a diamond. Imagine the diamond to be solid, three dimensional. Now pierce a hole through the centre of this. That hole, that passage is me. I am the link between the shores washed by the Caribbean sea, a hole, yet I am what joins your left hand to your right. I join the world of the living and the world of the spirits. I join the past with the present. In me Louise and Sue Ann are joined. Say Suzie Anna as Louise calls Mammy. Do you hear Louisiana there? Now say Lowly as Mammy calls Louise and follow that with Anna as Louise sometimes calls Mammy. Lowly-Anna. There's Louisiana again, particularly if you are lisp-tongued as you could well be. Or you could be Spanish and speak of those two venerable sisters as Louise y Anna. I was called in Louisiana, a state in the USA. Sue Ann lived in St Mary, Louisiana, and Louise in St Mary, Louisiana, Jamaica. Ben is from there too. I am Louisiana. I wear a solid pendant with a hole through its centre. I look through this hole and I can see things. Still I am Mrs Ella Kohl, married to a half-caste Congolese reared in Antwerp by a fairy godfather. I wear long loose fitting white dresses in summer and long black robes over them in winter. I am Louisiana. I give people their history. I serve God and the venerable sisters.

Den ah who seh Sammy dead

November 1946

Ten years of marriage to this lover and no need for maternity wear. "I wouldn't make a good father anyhow", he says. "I wouldn't give up my lifestyle." He does travel a lot. Often to Chicago. I think we have shares there in a salon or guest house or some such thing. "Where would you get the time to be a single mother?" he asks me. Truly I am busy. Madam Marie passed on and left her burdens to me. I now have all her West Indian men. Natives are coming to me too. My head is a cardboard box of US and West Indian file cards, each beginning 'name, date of birth, place of birth'. There are so many Grants on both sides, so many Walkers, Harrises, Forbes and so many towns with the same names that I am having a great deal of difficulty in separating my West Indians from my Americans. That is my problem; they seem quite able to make use of the history I hand them. I must be getting something right or why does my practice grow!

I am not Madam Marie. I don't engage my clients in arguments about the origins of their relationships with the songs they sing. I am Louisiana. After ten or so years with this clientele I know the songs and where we each learnt them. No need for argument. The songs are equally ours now. We just sing. I made no statement on this. It is the shape of things. My clients, though they are as many natives as West Indians, don't argue among themselves about origins either. I first noticed this funny departure with 'Prim strim stramma diddle'. Sheer nonsense if you ask me, but a common chord. The West Indian who had introduced it, had prefaced: "I learnt this song from the blackest man I have ever seen. It was as if someone had painted him in tar. He was from Barbados. A Baptist parson. He had served in West Africa." A man from Virginia said that he had no doubt that he had seen the very blackest man. He too was a parson who had been to Africa and was originally from the islands. Could the song be:

Coy me menero
kill Tukero
Coy mi nearo
Coy me
Prim strim stamma diddle
Lara bone a ring
Ting a rignum
Bulli dina coy me.

It was. Total nonsense. But there it was. A common chord. We hushed up after that.

With Madam's side vacant, we have space. Reuben has moved his business there. Into my parlour come the organised sounds of professionals rehearsing and the barriers do break, for the royalty of the jazz world grace us with their singing presence every now and then and the singing in my parlour of the US-West Indian men has more than once been the inspiration for a jazz work. Come to think of it, I am really doing a lot, as my husband says. "What you do is the matrix of many things", he tells me. It doesn't spell 'mother' though. Nor does it really spell 'horse'. And I had feared that I would be ridden to death by the venerable sisters!

Late 1946-1947

Let the record show that Louisiana, Ella Kohl, the former Ella Townsend made every effort to return the recording machine of the project to its rightful owners.

Nobody at Columbia knew me or was even aware that I had been given such an implement. The WPA project? Oh that! Did they know of it or were they humouring me. I don't know. It was indeed many years ago and I was speaking to a secretary who was speaking to someone else. The director of social research wouldn't even see me. The security officer attached to the building to which the door man had directed me, on a wink from the secretary, kindly I must say for both of them, showed me the door after the one-sided exchange in which I described my former involvement with the programme, how I had been given this machine, how it was many years after but that I'd like to speak to the relevant officer and formally return the instrument. "Perfectly alright", they said ever so politely, "we don't at all mind if you continue to keep it." The voice had sugar in it. It didn't want the tape recorder. No one wanted the tape recorder. Not even the juvenile rehabilitation centre. "Too old", they said, "the children would have difficulty handling it." I left it in the garbage by their gate. I hope some electronic minded juvenile finds it and learns something from it that will help to set him straight. Reuben has advised me, nay bade me to record this. "The world must know that use, not possession of the instrument is what you were about and that you tried to return it when you no longer needed it."

Since Louise related the initial segment of her story more than eight years ago, I have not used the recording machine. As a matter of fact since I named myself Louisiana the sisters have not conducted conversation with me via the machine. I like to feel that there is some promotion in that for me. They have been making contact with me via the pendant that I designed and which Reuben got a jeweller to execute. Much better. I have never been happy holding something that was not mine, and satisfied that all involved had made the switch from machine to pendant, from just

131

talking, to talking and seeing, I determined to return the thing to where it rightfully belongs and to get it out of my life at the first opportunity. That came with the call to New York. I had forgiven my parents long ago and had opened dialogue with them. Another one sided affair. "Ye who are without sin, cast the first stone", Madam had said out of the blue to me one day. And who did not know about honouring 'thy mother and thy father that thy days may be long in this land'? I wrote them at Christmas and on my birthday of the following year and thereafter religiously every year. I told them what I was doing. When I became Louisiana, I sent them a picture of myself. There was always a ps. "Tell me whether what I have seen of my early life is really so."

That sounds self-righteous. Hitting them with flowers. I can see that now as I write it down. But we could not sweep this thing under the carpet. I had no animosity, but for their mental health, the issue needed to be aired. Self righteous again, so let me be self-interested. Better? I plead for me. What was felt only by me could not be corroborated by them — I could not expect that, but certainly they could tell me whether Mass Bobby did keep me and how long after my grandmother's death they did arrive and so on. Surely they must be able to see that I needed to thank someone. They chose not to respond. Of course I cannot swear that they got my letters. Could be someone else took them and kept them. To blackmail my poor parents. The letters were never returned to sender. Or they could have both died in a fire and my letters with them. If my parents had passed on, then theirs would have to be the most finished deaths ever for nowhere in the region that I was permitted to traverse did I find one note in words or music on them. So I didn't know what to expect when I set off to New York to the lawyer's office from which the summoning note had come asking me to attend at their offices to discuss a matter affecting my parents and I.

The lawyer's first glance at me told a tale. I was something the cat had deposited on the mat. A chewed up rat. It had never struck me, nor did it Reuben, that to enter this part of America I would have to discard garments I had been wearing for years and find myself a more passable costume. The people with me in the train hadn't minded my outfit. Nor did those on the other side of Mr Lukas' office door there in Harlem. Ofcourse we were all black and therefore odd to begin with, so what did a dress a little bit more loose and a little longer than the others matter. Not so with Mr Lukas. He had seen me — I hesitate to say 'known' me — as a child. My mother had nursed his wife, and proud of me, Mother had taken me to see them on several occasions and as is the wont, they had handed down books, clothes and so on to me. At my entrance, Mr Lukas turned cherry pink and I knew that it wasn't because I had grown into a big girl, so I asked myself, could my blouse be open? Of course not. I do not wear buttons. My gowns go on over my head. Could my breasts be protruding and embarrassing the poor man? Nonsense. They haven't so much as touched the fabric of my dress for years so they couldn't make that kind of impression, my gowns are that loose. Mr Lukas regained his composure and said, "So you are now what? Nerf what, or didn't I get it straight?"

There and then I understood that for this world that I had once inhabited and had had to leave, I was mad. Benignly so for those at the Social research office in Columbia and for the superintendent of the juvenile home close by it. Mr Lukas was more analytical than my first institutional contacts and less kind. Madness is sin. It is the not doing of what ought to be done. It is turning right upon its head and calling it wrong. It is a woman standing on her head in her loose garments and exposing her nakedness for the world to see. It is pulling down one's father's pants,

133

pulling one's mother's skirts up to her waist. It is rejecting all that has been done for you. It is assuming your own position without embarrassment. Sin had entered Mr Lukas' space in the form of one Ella Kohl, now called Louisiana, the former Ella Townsend. The heat of its lair which she brought with her was what reddened the dear man's cheeks. I knew then — he didn't have to tell me — that there was no record of a missing recording machine at Columbia. Through him my parents had somehow paid for that first-edition-and-difficult-to-replace gadget and had paid off whatever else was necessary to expunge me and my history from their records. They had ofcourse left the oral reports and the whispers which would not come out of the corners to be fought and corrected. This thought put me in Mr Lukas' corner. Both of us unhappy. We faced each other with a common determination — to have this interview over as fast as possible, I, so I could weep for distorted history and he, to fumigate his office.

My parents, the lawyer and his documents said, had sold their properties and gone to retire in Jamaica. He offered me no addresses. I asked for none. Nor was there any letter discussing my early youth. There was a balance sheet which Mr Lukas pushed across to me — the duplicate thereof — and proceeded in his dry lawyer's style to read the details from the true copy. X amount had been put into the bank from when — a date even before they had come to take me to this place, if I remember rightly, and apparently sent from a foreign place. By x months, by x years at x percentage, it had become 2xy. Then there were the shares in c, which they had bought for me when I was 16. The monetary reward I had won for elocution that same year had been invested with d bank. At x percent for x years both had accumulated by x to be 2cdx. Insurance came to 2x. Then came the deductions. That was interesting but we both passed it over as if it was one of the xes. To Columbia

University for missing recording machine, p. Lawyers' fees tx, leaving a sum of $2xy+2cdx+2x-p-tx$. He took a cheque out of the envelope in which his copy had been, held it up to me using the tips of both his thumbs and index fingers and slid it across the table to me. Our hands have yet to meet. That was his goodbye. I took my cue, made for the door, held it open, turned around, stood quietly so that he could know that I had not left but was waiting for his attention, got it, curtseyed, then took my leave of him: "Sin, Sir, like beauty, is in the eye of the beholder". Let him wear that in his ears to the third and fourth generation. The piercing was instant for I saw his ears redden. I curtseyed again and took my leave of that part of my life.

What an odd resolution. They were really odd beings. My parents and the lawyer. They really suited each other. Money. Well money didn't kill anybody unless it fell in great heaps on them or unless they swallowed it. This was a cheque and I did not intend to eat it.

My teachers have never left me. Nor has Ben. He keeps me informed about happenings on his side of the road and that is how I came to know that my goodly parents were fine; had checked themselves into the country's most lavish nursing home and, as Ben puts it, were 'living the life of Riley'. I totally approved. I respected their wishes; I kept myself removed from them but never away from them. Ben is making arrangements for me to correspond with their priest. Ben himself is in fine shape. He did what I knew he couldn't avoid doing. He went back to Louisiana and confronted his past. He had lands there and is going into cows. Mass Bobby is no more, so there goes my hope of saying thanks to him while he is on this sod. That Miss Ros, his wife, my surrogate mother has disappeared with her children is all the news of the rest of the family that he can give me. Gone back to her family's land over the hills in Manchester, is all the villagers can tell him. But I know Ben

135

and before long Ros will be found and we will be in touch.

We. I gather from Reuben that we are quite wealthy. My cheque has added to our great wealth. We are into recording now. Not the kind I do. The production of music on disc. Discs like Silas used to play on his victrola only they don't use victrolas now. There is some story about seized property in Antwerp being returned to him with the end of the war and of Hitler, so Dame Fortune has piled two heaps of money suddenly on either side of what we had. I don't too much care for this wealth. I am still wearing white in summer and black in winter; my pendant still hangs on my chest. I still sew my clothes, make my vegetable gumbo, do my marketing on Wednesdays and tell my clients about their past most other days. It would be a double misfortune if my idle thought backfired on me and this heap of money fell over on me. I am thinking that we could reduce this pile by finding our way to the Congo. I don't know what will happen to my practice but if I can go off to New York for a few days, I suppose that I can go off to the Congo for three months. It is time. Then ofcourse I need to put aside something for Mass Bobby's children. Many if they are still alive and I hope they are so and remain so.

I look through my pendant often these days. I see heaven. You have to have a stout heart to go there, I am convinced. From where I look, things seem out of proportion and functions seem skewed. The moon for instance is a giant tablet. It must have some curative or life preserving value for I see folks breaking off bits and eating it. Thus I suppose full moon, half moon, quarter moon and then no moon. Ofcourse it grows back. The venerable sisters are ever so busy. Heaven is one large Chicago kitchen with no winter, no extreme summers and no mistress over them. I turn my pendant to them and watch much as the children are now watching images in comic books. A shadowy man is now appearing there with them and more and more I am hearing the 'voice': "*It is the voice I hear / the gentle voice I hear*" and I want to be with them.

December 1948

Reuben saw me holding on to the staircase to steady myself and claims that I am exhausted and need help. He has got me a maid. I ran away from her and went to the market. I know enough to know when it is Wednesday, what does that man think? I slipped away again and am here with those white-coated people. I don't know why Lowly and Sue Ann have chosen to appear in those garbs. That's their business. At least they have finally brought Silas with them, and my Reuben, who is really quite nice when he has the time, has brought me pen and paper.

–What's so great about you that your story has been kept away from me– I ask him. –Did these sisters think I would steal you away?– He smiles shyly. Got to get him to talk.

I fell down the stairs and broke my leg. I am distressed. I am grounded. I am separated from the upper rooms of my house and the lower. I cannot go out to the vegetable market. I cannot make my stew. Reuben has got me help and I meekly take it this time. This cast itches like hell. It should be off already. There is something about my foot not having healed properly and needing to be set all over again. Reuben is worried. Why did I fall, he and the doctor are asking me? "I guess I tripped over my skirts, they are long you know." He isn't satisfied. "They have been long these ten years and you haven't tripped." "What wasn't done in ten years is done in a day", I say but their bother bothers me. Lurline is good enough. After my recovery we'll send her to learn touch typing. My husband is on to me to pull all my stuff together and write. It makes sense particularly with all the time I have on my hands but am I now that kind? I am jotting down something every day. It hasn't worked before, but then I didn't have a broken leg in a fat

137

white cast that will keep me from moving for six weeks or more.

Mardi gras has just passed by. I sewed. Far more than any other year. Because I am laid up with a broken leg. Poor Reuben. He has to be a New World Zulu again for I cannot travel with this leg and he says he won't leave the USA without me. Now that the sewing is over, I should really organise myself into collecting the bits and pieces and organising them according to files. I have been jotting in different note books and on odd bits of paper and throwing them willy nilly into my desk drawer. One good point for me. At least I know where to find them. Perhaps if Reuben would stop urging me, I would get on with the work. Actually I am far more interested in what is going on with him than in going on with my work. Is my compere par excellence tired of the bright lights and trying to worm his way back into academia? "No. Just trying to re-live those days of yesteryear when we were so close in a cabin in St Mary, Louisiana. And dammit, you were a writer. I met you as a writer." Well, well. This is the man who couldn't understand my resistance to being a hoodoo woman. I am now as close to that as I can get. "Stop teasing", he says, "You know this is no hoodoo. This is… " I wait. "Give it a name, Sir", I continue to tease him. "Jung" he starts. I stop him. "Reuben", I say? "you have not visited with those minds for close on ten years. I cannot live your life for you." It seems we are to change our trajectory a bit, or has our journey been completed?

January 1949

The cast is off but we are definitely keeping Lurline on. She can dust and clean. I have taken back my marketing chores and vegetable gumbo Louisiana style — that's me — is back, so is the sadness then laughter of my men. The extra time granted me by Lurline's presence is now spent in the little library that is available to our kind. I need to get as much information on South West Louisiana as I can. What would be in their library anyhow?

February 1949
The Teche Strike

As I am writing this Mammy is laughing at me. Information on the Teche strike in the library? News of my mother in the library? Where else Mammy? Who laughs last ... I checked the University that our folks are trying to establish, have established really and Mammy, I can tell you the date of that disturbance. 1878. It didn't actually say, 'strike-in-which-Mammy's-mother-took-part'. "Disturbance in the canefield" is what it said. So there. I don't know where to find the details. The newspaper reports did not list the names of the participants. It did say though that women as well as men were involved in leadership roles, so that's the evidence that your mother's action has been recorded for posterity. What does the search prove? I don't know that it says anything more than you have said, but it does help that you are not the only person who says what you say, that people to whom you haven't spoken verify what you have said. You didn't tell me when you were born. My search did. You were born shortly before that strike, you tell me. You were therefore born late 1877 or early 1878. I could ask the old people who were around at the time to give me some leads to the names but you are right, what your granny felt, what your mother felt, what you felt cannot be told any better than you have told it. I do not doubt you Mammy, nor any of the things you said, and for me, even if what you relate did not happen to you, it happened to someone's granny, someone's mother. Someone. Some baby was hurt. Please don't make me cry. I know why myself was chosen to write the story you dictate. I have been there too. Chimboraza, Cotapaxi took me by the hand.

139

April 1949

I am saddened. I have been sitting down in my chair saddened. I think that for the very first time I have found my way into the depths of Mammy's sadness. Reuben has begun his Chicago runs again and I am glad. He watches me like a hawk. My sadness could have him sending for the doctor. He is pleased to see me listening and recording. Let that be what he sees. Is there anything I want to check in the Chicago archives? What is going on with him? Relax Reuben.

December 1949

I lost my balance in the study and fell. I must have hit my head against something for I blacked out. The doctor says I should send for my husband. I will not. I am alright again but I will take this rest.

"The doctor thinks that your broken leg and now your fall and black-out mean that you are over-stressed. I am ordering rest. I am putting you on leave from your practice. You will write and do your vegetable stew only. Lurline knows your contacts in the market. You can send messages to them." The big man has spoke. "Honey I'm getting frightened." You sure are, my big man.

February 1950

With nothing to do but write and do my vegetable stew I fell down the stairs again before I could settle into anything. I am in bed. They say I have dislocated my hip and the doctor and Reuben now exchange glances behind my back. Looks like a general conspiracy for those two moon-eating sisters of mine are there with them too. *It is the voice I hear...*

Whom do they think they are fooling? This whole battery of tests and Reuben neglecting his business and looking at me like a besotted poet. The venerable two have been outplayed too. If they had ever thought they were the last word, now they know they aren't. "Don't say you are not the Christ!" Don't say. Hmmmm. Now. They are rushing frantically around like midwives about to lose a baby, rushing in without even the usual signature. I have entered my 40's. Lowly went at what? 20 something. Rushing to prepare me my place but let it be told in Gath, I am not ready. I shall not go until I have made a closer acquaintance with one or more of the fathers.

"He helped to make things happen."

"Too capsulated", I say and "he who?" I know they're trying to rush me.

"Reuben", I say, "I am glad I have said more about you than that you helped to make things happen." The other repeats,

"He helped to make things happen."

"That's not enough", I say. The pictures are blurred with the grey eminences barely filtering through. I can't make out whether there are more than one, whether there is Ramrod and Silas and who else. "Clarity", I say.

"Write quickly", they say. Reuben and Lurline are here. He to write, she to type.

Lowly talks first.

−He was Colthurst again. An older version. He never touched me. He taught me other things.− In her haste she can still stop to smile coquettishly at her older sister. I am transported to that Chicago kitchen. She repeats for emphasis, "He never touched me". Accent on the me.

−Oh yes I touched you alright− that voice which I have heard just once before and only as a smile comes in. −Little gal from the islands searching for a manageable Colthurst. What a blotting paper you were child, soaking up all them stories of Cuba and Colon. How you wanted to hear of Africa "where I come from". What a thirst! I guess with no live mother and father, your personal history knew no boundary. That's what set me roving too. You in your head, me with my feet. Could be just a land of loud-mouthed sunshine you were looking for though back there in that Chicago cold. Whatever it was, you forced me to think. Not just more, deeper. You dragged everything from me that Cuba had told me about. Chicago had forced race on you. Never knew that there was somewhere a whole world of people who looked like Father and so few who looked like you, searching anywhichway for that world of yours. You forced me to add, to think, to add to Matanza's story of the coming of the Africans to Cuba and why, though I spoke no Spanish and they no English, there were common words between us.–

–And you sent me back home. Say that too. To get me out of the way.–

–That lady there is another story– I could see Louisiana smiling. I guess she could hear the smile in his voice and the tease in Mammy's as she entered with a "Yeah?"

–Faded photograph!– the male voice continued.

–Honey I apologised– Mammy's voice came in again. I knew it well. But with deference? That must be new even to Lowly.

–Honey I tell you over again, there's nothing to apologise for. Can't apologise for carrying around a faded photograph of the man you love. Can't say I'm complaining or ever did, about replacing your father. Just wish you'd made the switch earlier. Woman wait almost until the Arkansas contrariness carry me away.–

March 1950

This is a natural pause. My wife stopped speaking and rested for a good many days. I take the opportunity given by this break to explain the presence of my voice in this manuscript.

142

If you have read this far, you know that I have training in Anthropology. I have not worked seriously in this area for more than 15 years but there are precepts which remain with me. Faithfully represent the field is one of these. The field now includes me in a way it never did before. After the pendant and before this last onset of illness, the conversation between Louisiana and her otherworld people was a private affair between them: they spoke in her head; she wrote what they said. I heard nothing and knew nothing excepting for that which she shared with me. Now conversation still takes place in her head but it is expressed through her speaking organs. I put it this way to underline the fact that it is not Louisiana's voice that I, the scribe hear. She is neither reporting speech nor translating. The voices I hear, are as with the recording machine, those of other people. I, ofcourse recognise Mammy's voice. I, as I have said, am merely the scribe. I don't know how long I can be this and remain emotionally detached but I certainly shall record my involvement as soon as I am aware of it. As of now, refurbishing the shorthand which I was forced to learn in my early preparation for fieldwork, I record on paper what comes out of my wife's mouth. I de-cipher and pass this on to Lurline who does a typescript. I know my wife's spirit. There are going to be days when she insists on doing her recordings by herself. I'll let her. Then I'll have time to do what I have been doing since the voices stopped — collate the bits of paper on which she has hitherto done her transcriptions and organise these in the sequence in which I think they were revealed to her, along with her commentaries.

April 1950

Louisiana is up again. She thinks she is back on her feet but she isn't. Her hands shake, and pressing her fingers around the pencil is torture. I suppose that I will definitely be invested as scribe. I will not intrude. I will not offer my services. Let her call.

June 1950

As if there had not been this break, the session continues. It is the voice of Silas, I learn. Mammy's husband. He continues.

–That feisty lady there was always trying to stop the kid from coming to my room.–

–Man see you peeping, take his finger call you. Man never said right and proper like he should, 'Miss Sue Ann, would you like to come in and listen to some music?' Ain't fitting for the boarders to mix like that with the maids, and glancing around when he pass through the kitchen, like he and I have something going.– Louisiana was laughing. She was amused by the image of this earlier Mammy falling clumsily in love and even in the retelling handling it so clumsily. I smiled but what I felt like doing was crying. It had been so many years since we had laughed together. I don't now have a quaint language for her to laugh at. So much has passed. And now...

–Woman barge into my room ready to beat me up. "What's wrong with this child's skin you have her spending her money on bleaching cream?" I am dumbfounded but I don't protest. She is in my room. And I love the look of anger. I don't know what she see in this face of mine but before I can take in more of this closeness, the woman stop suddenly in her tracks, and backs away through the door. Old photograph get up and bowing like the skinny ear of corn in Joseph's dream must be frighten her. I had heard her tell the child that I was nothing but an old faded photograph. Old photograph breathing frighten this lady. Now it is a whole set of hanging down of head and stiffer silence when I walk through the kitchen. This old photograph never feel

144

so powerful before! I corner the child and hand her a lecture:

Fleecy locks nor dark complexion
Cannot forfeit nature's claim—

—I never forget that Silas (Lowly speaking). And thank me here and now. If I didn't send off for the skin bleach, you'd never have married Sue Ann. "Girl you got to get me out of this", you said, and I did. It was when I told her of the ads in the newspaper and of what we talked about in your room that she started to see merit in you. "You want to tell me island baby that a man like that, so ready as you say, is prepared to carry that machine from which part of foreign it come from to sing and play them dirty words:

Coon, coon, coon
I wish my colour would fade
Coon, coon, coon
To be a different shade
Coon, coon, coon
Morning noon and night
I'd rather be a whiteman
'Stead of coon, coon, coon."

—Then you explained to me according to what he said: "If you are afraid of what people call you, then they have power over you. They call you 'coon', then call yourself 'coon'. You now have power over the name. When next you hear that song, say to yourself, 'the coon can'."
—"Made sense" you said, then she couldn't get enough answers.—
—Still my old lady here not saying a word to me. Head bow down further, stiffer silence when I pass. You'd think the lady would ups and apologise.—
—I was too ashamed— a penitent Mammy said —Anyways, Silas, that ain't no fitting song— Our Mammy still had the

last word.

–You right my lady.– Silas merely placed the period to her sentence.

That trio must have had a grand time.

July 1950

What was our beginning like? Dammit, I can't remember. I like this Silas. If it were in my power to do so, I would hasten the telling because I want to hear his story and because I want Louisiana to stop this session of conveying so that we too can go back into our past and have some fun before the end.

December 1950

She is so skinny. Even I can feel their presence and hear the song. *It is the voice I hear*… I am so afraid. I wish I could share the pain or that it would all end. What is she waiting for? Most of her time now is spent in bed. It is my privilege to hold her hand, my duty to write. We both see that. I do both. So I am an extension of the bed. In this way I can switch from lover to scribe as is necessary. Just as well for it is in snatches that the voices come. The body can bear only just that much.

January 1951

–Then was when we became a trio–

February 1952

Nothing more for several days. It was Silas' voice again.

–All of 1920 we studied. (Silas is speaking)–
–I have never liked it that you gave up learning to make eye-glasses and went to work on that killing floor– that's Mammy's voice.
–Lady I was humble before the story of you in that waterfront strike and having the foresight to flee Louisiana so you could live to fight another day. And the way you

146

came to that knowledge! I wanted to be the one who put your pot on the fire Mam. It's been nothing but my pleasure, Mam.–

April 1952

Louisiana's own voice is very low. What she wants to say to me of our own business or her business, is said in whispers, my ear to her mouth. The forces have all her energy. I can hear them quite clearly. She indicated during this session that I should come closer. "Good", she said. I suppose she feels she has struck pay dirt — something more on Mammy's history. Still working for Columbia and the WPA, she is! Can't shake the guilt.

–Meeting you Silas was like drawing water off of the head– Mammy says. –Forget about the photograph. There was that too but that was juvenile business. A big old 40 year old Mamma searching for her father! And I didn't even know I was. Just saw that picture jumping when I accused you of that thing in your room. The flight out of New Orleans, the fear, the sadness and tears on that chicken bone special, the feeling that I was abandoning ship, the cloud, the persistent cloud, in Chicago and loneliness made sense. Look where I come to learn what I should learn in grade school, to read newspapers, to know what is going on all over the world.–

–I didn't teach you anything else?–

–At forty! Where you was before that man. Come changing my life at forty. Couldn't you have come before and given us some more time?–

–Bad boy.–

–Yes. Your fault. Walk too slow, Man. And couldn't even stick around for ten years!–

–You. Lady, you didn't need more than ten years. In that little space of time you lived fifty years. Found you could tune in and hear things, found you could make two babies.

Found Mr G and how to get home. Organising in the dead of night, sneaking here, setting up meeting there, carrying all those quarters people on your head. Good thing your own kids went home. 'Sue Ann what me must do with Jeanie?' 'Sue Ann, hold back the river, bring the moon.' This woman, she and Marie, even after Mr G left, wanting to pull the sides of the sea together, wanting to sew them little islands together and tack them on to New Orleans. Them and that tavern! "Women", I say, "Why can't you make quilt from scraps like other women?" "The work", they say, "Gotta do the work what with him gone." And I just a mere man could not resist them. Work my soul case to smithereens til I think God switch the sign on me and have me in hell rather than in heaven. Would the woman come home and give me some peace! And Mam. Me. Had my soul and body serving you even after death though the man we stood before only said, "Til death". So glad the girl turned up. Still she be my lady.–

You-know-who-would-do-it whispers, "G=Garvey".

So. So. There it is. Finally out. I looked at Louisiana. She was smiling. That was Mammy and how she came to be of interest to those looking for the history of the black people of South West Louisiana. Not even fifteen minutes. Louisiana had waited and waited, must be, fifteen years for this. Mammy was a Garvey organiser and a psychic. We had long known about the latter. A black nationalist. Well, well, well. "The units", Louisiana mumbled. 'What units did she set up?', Louisiana had asked herself over and over. Why couldn't the answer have surfaced before? Why couldn't someone in St Mary have mentioned it? Why couldn't Madam Marie have said it? Cryptic Marie had answered: "He who feels it knows it", meaning I suppose, 'it will be revealed to you when you are emotionally there' and our/her seeking had ceased. They didn't want to talk of it.

People's memories of events close in time to them, is poor. Poorer still if it is a painful memory. They don't want to remember. The failure as it apparently was in this case, is just so painful and difficult to handle. It inhibits analysis. And putting words on things means analysis. People share post analysis. They file things away until their emotions can deal with them. Twenty years time will find them laughing and talking about what they chose to forget today. Until then, those who want to know must 'feel' their way to it. And hasn't she 'felt' her way to it!

I half expect that my wife now that she knows what she wants to know, will now close her eyes and join your heavenly throng. Grieve for me Silas.

May 1952

Louisiana is recovering. Dare I believe that the doctor is wrong?

June 1952

Dare I believe that the doctor is wrong. Her colour is back; the pain seems to be gone; she is putting on weight and walking around, hesitantly but still walking.

August 1952

I have been reading Reuben's recordings. Seems to have been a close shave. From his point of view ofcourse. From mine it was more like a long rest. I can't even remember the pain he thinks I felt. Only at the very beginning. Perhaps I lost consciousness. I don't know. What I recall is being with them and hearing them tell their story/stories. It is down on paper and in Reuben's hand so I must have been a speaking conduit. I am here now in the world Reuben occupies. I don't know what any of this means for if the truth be known, I was as comfortable there as here. I am here now and I shall be as good as can be here. I will continue to keep the diary, certainly to record sequentially and regularly.

I'll do as Reuben wishes. I will not go to the market; I will not see clients; I will write; I will rest. The doctor has nothing to say about my return save, "It happens". "Rest", he says. I will rest.

November 1952

I have reviewed the collection — transcripts and commentaries in all its totality. All the pieces I can recall receiving and writing are in and in order. Reuben did a good job. His comments deserve inclusion. I think I'll now do a sketch of Mammy.

December 1952

Mrs Sue Ann Grant-King was born around 1878 to a mother who was separated, perhaps abandoned by her husband, the father of her unborn child. The gestation period was an unhappy one for the mother and I suppose the child in her womb. Apart from not knowing the whereabouts of her recent groom and not having been left anything else of him but a photograph album of pictures mainly of him and of her wedding day, Mrs Grant, Mammy's mother had little emotional support from her own mother with whom the young pregnant wife had to live and who disapproved of her choice of mate. It is hardly likely that she would have had alternative sources of emotional support within the village of St Mary, Louisiana, to which she had returned after her whirlwind courtship in New Orleans, because no one there knew her husband and they quite likely had supported the candidacy of her creole suitor who was known to be a good man, economically sound and in every way a good catch. For young Mrs Grant, born about 1862 and therefore in her teens at the time, carrying her child and the circumstances surrounding it, were a burden which plunged her into a depression. With the birth of the child the depression lifted. Mrs Grant appeared to understand that the support and the upbringing of the child depended solely on her and immersed herself into the only gainful employment that was available to her kind — field work in sugar cane. It appears that she worked harder than was necessary, perhaps looking for activity which could help her forget the past. Whatever... she worked demonaically hard, gaining the respects of all colleagues to the point where they allowed her to take on the additional task of organising them towards wresting a better deal from sugar planters. The focus of action of Mrs Grant and her co-conspirators was better pay and the modification of a system of remuneration in which workers were forced to spend their wages in the company stores owned by the same plantation owners and from which debts were deducted before the pay reached the hand of the worker. Enough has been written on this subject of manufactured bills, of the impossibility of balancing budgets, of having to hand over stock and real estate to the planters to cover these fictitious bills. Suffice it to say that Mrs Grant saw her inherited substance, a small plot of land, nursed and handed down in the family, about to fall into the planters' hands, her debts being said to be larger than her wages. This young woman's end is not really known. It is the general assumption that she was disposed of by the planters because of her political activities. Such an end would make her the third person in her family to have been thus engaged and to have met such an end. Her father had been lynched shortly before emancipation and perhaps before she was born. A similar fate met her step father who was the father she knew.

This is the family culture in which Mammy grew — punished resistance. She grew with her grandmother, truly a woman of sorrows who by this sad fact achieved some notoriety in the area. No one wanted to add to her martydom, if it could at all be helped. They resented her status. No one wanted to see another resistance and another punishment in that family. The village and its leading lights did not want their shame to re-surface every generation. This family was the living proof of their cannibalism. The village wanted a new press. Consciousness about its image must have gone a far way to creating a kind of goodwill which somehow led Mammy out of Nebuchadnezzar's fiery furnace, for she like her forebears was incapable of not thinking about social conditions and trying to change them. 'You can kill the body. That's happened before and we are still here.' The incipient labour movement of the pre-World War I days was Mammy's stage, her chance to perpetuate the family tradition. She became involved in New Orleans in the longshoreman's strike. What actually inspired her to withdraw from this and make for Chicago has yet to be revealed, but she appears to have left in haste as much possibly from a tip that the axe was about to fall as possibly from a feeling that it was now time for somebody from that family to stay alive and effect change from this side of the world.

Mammy appears to have been apolitical in Chicago until she met and was courted by Silas King. King had travelled widely and been one of the preening contingent of black Chicagoans who had distinguished themselves in the First World War. He was trying to become an optometrist. In Chicago she also met Louise Grant who was a young Jamaican orphan, fairly well educated in the literary arts and domestic science for a woman of her class, colour and times. They worked as kitchen staff in a guest house. Silas King was a boarder. He undertook the political socialisation of the young orphan. Mammy eventually joined their efforts at education and in the process upgraded her literary skills. Here she seemed also to have developed her gift for second sight. These three devoted themselves to informing themselves about happenings in the black world and to developing strategies for changing this world. Their discovery of the man who was to make such an impact on the minds of black folks, Marcus Garvey, brought them a clearer focus. His UNIA gave them a framework within which to do concrete work. Silas and Mammy produced two children possibly before leaving Chicago and returned to St Mary, Louisiana, where she and perhaps he as well, did organisational work. Silas died, the children died and Mammy was left alone. She continued her political work intertwining it with her psychic work, a combination which served to make her a legend.

Re-read. Here then is this little bit of story. Did Prof know any more than this? I doubt it. Who now wants to know. I don't much care. There it is. Anyhow, I am tired.

April 1953

Such a long time since I heard our signature tune that I hardly recognised it. It is soft. I take this as a cue to doing nothing about it. The reason? I want to spend some more time with my husband. Wish we could make it to the Congo. I won't even ask. Reuben would not consider it. "You need to build back your body" and ofcourse he is right. Not only do I need to build back my body, I need to have some fun with this man. I'm jazzing now and really 'into it' as they say here. Mercy, it is great. New Orleans is a wonderful musical city.

May 1953

Good news from Ben. One of Mass Bobby's sons has won a scholarship. Must be a great achievement. Ben makes it sound like that. Will ofcourse do my part. The pater and the mater are better than I, according to Ben. Hale and hearty. I must take a leaf out of their book and live the high life.

June 1953

Ah who say Sammy dead. Very strong this time. They are here again and ready. With the rest and the fun of the past months, I am thinking of being accommodating.

153

Things have certainly changed. "Accommodating." Fancy me saying that, being the accommodating one. My work must really be finished. Actually there are gaps that I'd like to fill and I do agree with Reuben that this transcript and these comments could be valuable. The bottle with the message thrown in the sea and found several millenia after. But seriously, it could give guides to researchers. I don't think for instance that the nature or extent of the influence of black America on the Caribbean and vice versa has been explored as it should. I have no doubt that the acculterating relationship of those three in that Chicago kitchen was duplicated all over the place and certainly that man Garvey who extrapolated these relationships into a movement ought to be looked at by scholars.

July 1953

"Yes" says Lowly, the most academic of the three. It is she who wants to come in. I'll certainly make time for her. I feel sorry for that kid side-lined by the lovers in that Chicago kitchen.

–I wasn't side-lined. No. I really wasn't– Lowly glided in. –When talking began between Silas and Sue Ann, more activity for me came with it. We went places together. Silas took us places. I'd been caged in that house before. We talked a lot. I helped to teach Sue Ann. Sue Ann taught Silas and me certain things. We taught each other many things. For instance, Silas took books by mail. He was interested in the mind, telepathy and that whole area of mind control, of outer body experiences. As we talked about his reading, Mammy became aware of like experiences she had had. She talked about these. She had never talked about them before. A significant one was her coming to Chicago. She had been thick into the longshoreman's strike. Like happened to the prophets in the Bible, a voice came to her, a hand touched her on the shoulder and guided her

154

away to the train. Somebody out of the blue paid her fare. News came after of the shooting and jailing of the strikers. She could never explain to herself how she had left something that was vital to her and in such a flash. There had been guilt but with our reading and talking, she was now seeing herself as selected by a higher authority to have a set of experiences different from that of her relatives and selected for another task. Whoever controlled the world she now felt, had said that enough of her line had been wasted in battle, that she should take a new approach to fighting. Sue Ann's confession was instructive for me. I had never thought, before she spoke, that this kind of experience was a thing, was significant. I thought it was a feature of everyday existence. I did not know that I had been given a special gift. All of my life, small to theirs, I had had experiences of that kind. I saw myself because of Sue Ann's revelations and because of Silas reading and the understanding which he got from these readings, in a new light. Silas and his books taught us control. I could be tidying a bedroom and at the same time be talking to Sue Ann at the wash tub way down in the basement. We would need an explanation to something and Silas would materialise with the answer without being verbally summoned or asked. I wasn't left out at all. I was growing with them and through them.

–Obviously there were things which they did which didn't include me. They did try to teach me coon can but I never was good enough to go out and play against others in those Saturday night sessions which our people had throughout our side of the city. More active things must have taken place. I don't know where they would have the privacy for any such thing, so they must have taken place after my exit. It is true that they were instrumental in sending me home, but you must know that I was teasing: it was not to get me out of the way. Long before their speaking, Silas had advised me to go home. He loved to talk about 'karma' — the state of your being, it meant according to him. I had told him of Colthurst. "You need to go home and face him", he had said. "That experience is tarnishing your karma." I saw his point. That wasn't what sent me home though, although Silas was involved in the primary reasons. What put my first foot forward was the riot. You do know of the riots, don't you dear. 1919– I wasn't sure that I did, but Lowly would tell me.

–One of our boys swam out a little too close to the white side of the beach and they killed him. I'd been there in Chicago for about a year and until the speaking of Sue Ann and Silas, had seen nothing and known nothing. Such wickedness and race hate I had never met. Even with Sue Ann's telling of the shooting and jailings which she escaped, I had not grasped the sadness of this hatred. You could say the strikers hurt somebody by not doing work which they were expected to do, but a 14 year old boy swimming and accidentally going too far to one side! Unbelievable. Here it was at my door, closing down the whole town, keeping guests away from the guest house, having people whispering and walking with clubs. So much hatred all around. I forgot to be frightened; I was so angry.

–Silas smiled throughout the upheaval and throughout my surprise and anger. I can still remember his rebuke as if it was yesterday: "Little sister, ain't nothing abnormal about this. Happening in your home town too." I don't know if he saw this telepathically. Whatever the source, it was a fact. Some days later he showed me a newspaper — rioting on estates in my island, the names of which were familiar to me, if not exactly "my home town". We meditated on the similarities — all three of us. Me, Sue Ann and Silas. The second thing he said to my anger, said it in one of these meditative sessions was, "Anger is impotence. If you want to

156

change things you can. Make the change in your corner. The good Lord said, 'let your net down at your feet'. This is not your corner. What you do there, will be felt throughout the world for everything is related." Come to think of it I never did find out whether the Lord did say that and if He did, where he said it. Nevertheless, that speech was what put my first foot on the boat for home. The second foot followed through the newspaper business. I had read items to which he had pointed me in his newspapers. Glanced through them and other stuff he had not marked for my reading — that's how I found the advertisement for the bleaching cream which brought Sue Ann into our company. I began after his speech, to check the newspapers carefully, to question him about their origin, where printed, brought by whom and so forth. They were from places I had only heard of, places whose inhabitants I had never seen. Trinidad, for instance. Silas had travelled extensively but he had not been to Trinidad. I doubt whether he knew any Trinidadian either but here we were reading Trinidadian newspapers and knowing what was going in Trinidad. Silas has mentioned my capacity to ferret out information. I dug and dug until I was led to the organisation and Silas had no choice but to take us there. In that first room and those subsequent meetings that I attended there were people like us everywhere and only us; we had newspapers from everywhere. I heard the 'little black man from St Ann' and decided to put my spade down where I was born. But you are tired. Another time.–

August 1953

I had become really frail; frailty plus involvement with that story meant a very very tired me, but it was all so exciting. I had to share it with Reuben. Together we went over my rough transcriptions and over these transcriptions again and again until we had a perfect, lucid copy with the

157

punctuation marks in all the right places. We spent nearly a week on it. It was like the days of the cottage in St Mary. "Jesus", he said to me when we were finished, "this is a privilege. This really did happen and we have just made what I believe to be the only existing record of it."

I might have been foolhardy given the state of my health, but I called this time.

Have you ever seen a wound-up chug-chugging toy car with the key in its back or side or wherever, capsize, the key stuck in a hole in the floor or caught in the door or something and the car consequently frozen in action and in sound? Turn it over and it continues its programme without as much as an 'excuse my mishap'. That was Lowly. Only ingrained manners had made her note my frailty and my tiredness and stop. My poor health was the hole in the floor, the obstructing door. She had turned herself inside out for the first time I think, and could not return to herself until she had finished her story. If I had had doubts about my service to her, they were at an end. She needed to tell it out. Mr President's grant did not cover her. What would the poor young woman have done without me. There was a lesson somewhere in that for me to contemplate but more on that later. I must do what is urgently required and let the lady's tale take shape upon paper.

–Doors open on every side as soon as you take a committed position. I was an orphan, devoid not only of parents but of blood relations. I purposely say 'was'. That identity fell away from me in the organisation. There were so many hands and hearts ready to place me with their kith and kin that I could pick, choose and refuse. That Sue Ann there that you call Mammy, don't underestimate her. I know you don't but I feel I must say it. "Girl", she said, "you ain't going home to be nobody's chamber-maid or scullery girl. You going home to be a professional woman." I chose to do nursing. Sue Ann paid my fees to night school. I went home with my

158

nursing qualifications. 1921. No. Late 1920 and began working at the Kingston Public Hospital early 1921 as a ward maid. Sue Ann's sphere of influence did not stretch that far! It was a job. It paid for my keep. Most importantly, it kept me in the thick of things.–

They must have been listening. Taken time out from their moon-eating and cavorting to listen to her for the sound, "And we were proud", came in. "We heard about those speeches from Coke chapel steps — 'let it ring, let it ring, let it ring'." So Lowly was a speaker and a poet to boot!

Slight break. Lowly continues unmindful of the teasing.

–Then helping to form the cohort of nurses. We were absolutely necessary. As the crowds grew so did the demand for our skills. What a throng there was to see the Black Star Line. Kingston had never seen so many people. They came from the deepest wild, on every transportation there was. They walked. We helped to keep order as well as administering to the sick. We held each other's outstretched arms to form a cordon to keep the crowd from overflowing into the streets and hindering the progress of the parade of the crew and of the officers of the organisation. Hear the shout when Garvey appeared! That was something. We helped at other levels too. It was just as well that Kingston Public Hospital could only see me as a ward maid. It released my creative energies to serve the organisation. I worked too as a clerk, clipping newspaper items and filing them. I had a special love for that work: it kept me in touch with Sue Ann and Silas. Not that they were the subject of newspaper articles but to read was to be transported to the scene in Chicago in which they were active, and occasionally one of the seamen — the couriers were usually seamen — would have seen them or heard of them. Then ofcourse there was the other way of communicating. This was as

159

clear as a bell when they went to St Mary, Louisiana. Ehem, Ehem.– Lowly actually cleared her throat in that way people have of indicating that they are about to say a mischievous thing, before saying,

–With me out of the way they soared to heights so far up that mistress could see that her cook was 'messing' with her boarder. Who laughs last... –

Mammy must have been listening.

–Actually– she came in –the lady was quite considerate but with me pregnant, it stood to reason that I would have to go and news had already come by that the work was taking root back down home so we were quite ready to go, thank you Mam.– Mammy would have the last word!

–And listen to her talking so bold and strong– she continues. –Ups and dies so soon after she gets home. Had you all the way with me though baby. We moved, Louisiana.– First time I recall her calling me by that name or any name at all.

–She moves too back to her old Louisiana. We had some touching times then.–

–Don't forget I did do some work there. Didn't just sit connecting with you– Mammy went ahead, not waiting for a response.

–Old folks saw the flesh was tired, over-burdened. Called her home.–

October 1953

There was nothing more. I knew there was nothing more. Nothing more but for myself to understand why this was my experience. All that I had left to do was to meditate on this but in my meditation to leave space for pleasures with my mate. Going to Africa was out. I couldn't make it. Jamaica was closer. I might make it but what would this weak flesh do there? The planning of the trip alone would deplete my little store of energy. Better stay put and imagine and make

160

my husband's gumbo for as long as my strength allows. I feel this is the end.

November 1953

Very faint sound of the theme. It is Lowly. "You don't need to know about Colthurst, do you?" My sister is thorough! No I don't need to know. Political work was so satisfying, Colthurst melted.

Strong sounds. This is it. My chariot. Swing low. I hear it. I feel it.

January 1954

Pain. Bone breaking pain, shooting from my bones, silver bullets dead set on freedom, liberated, fill my room with lightning bugs and I am become Christmas, starlights, fireworks, holidays, no flesh. I have become a hot silver tree melted to a single conduit that courses through the gap above my temples from left to right, bending and fitting itself and doubling back to the centre of my pendant. I am a silver stethoscope. Anyday now that line will be a silver thread, a strand, will slip through my pendant, be a streak of lightning. What a relief then to be making my way over the rainbow's mist! Til then, I am a metal aerial conductor tuned to the rainbow and this is the day of pentecost. Must be.

A shorthand way of talking for she had very few words left, but talk about angel voices! My wife's voice was there too. Different chords, different tunes, different octaves. Sheer jazz. One sound. From one body. A community song: *It is the voice I hear, I hear them say, come unto me...* Louisiana, my wife, Ella Kohl, the former Ella Townsend, was smiling and singing. She was going over the rainbow's mist with her knowing smile. I know now what she knows: Mammy would not tell the president nor his men her tale for it was not hers; she was no hero. It was a tale of cooperative action; it was a community tale. We made it happen.

161

Epilogue

Coon Can

April 1954

I thought of taking her body to Jamaica. I knew just how the break or perhaps it is a failure to bond — whatever — with her parents hurt her. Messed with her karma as Silas would have put it. I felt that her burial in their island and hopefully with them present would be the best gift I could give her. Too much red tape. A body even of one so beautiful does not stay forever. Louis was my strength. He could not conceal his pleasure that my Jamaican plans had not worked. "She belongs here", he maintained. "She should have a real New Orleans funeral." The boys were all with him. I managed to secure a compromise. We would bury her in St Mary, Louisiana, New Orleans style. They were all there. "She did so much for the music", they said. I did not know that they too knew the extent to which the fusion of music of the island men and the natives seeped over into our rehearsal room and influenced us.

What a sight for St Mary's eyes. So many birds... Read her manuscript for yourself. I am no writer. What was said for Mammy and Lowly can be said for her. Just multiply by six. They played them for her in jazz style — *Sammy Dead* and *I hear the voice*... No other one got that.

I want to publish this manuscript. It is my wife's story too. It is the story of the conduit, the scribe as much as that of the actors. Her story needs to be told for, still troubled by the break between my wife and her parents and perhaps looking for earthly kin, I went to Jamaica. As far as I knew

165

then, I went to inform Louisiana's parents of her death. There I found that I was what they call a 'samfie man' who had led their daughter into 'lower class life'. It is necessary that Louisiana's manuscript see the light of day and correct this impression of her life and work. Her parents are here now. Perhaps they had planned it. I don't know, but by the time I reached back here to New Orleans there was Ben's letter saying that they had moved to Connecticut. Have they moved to be closer to her? I might be a romantic at heart. I, for my part intend to be a son-in-law to them as long as I am here, which might not be very long. There is marching again here. Protest is all about and our people are making their discontent known. Is this my community? Have I any business in this? I am hearing of Kasavubu and Lumumba. I am beginning to think that I must put down my spade in the Congo where I was born. Right, Silas. The prospect is exciting. That would be an extension of the community. Isn't that exciting! The coon can.